I0779618

This book is dedicated to my partner, Elizabeth for her continued support and faith and her love of all things wild.

Acknowledgments

I especially want to thank my editor Debbie Burke for finding clarity in my words and bringing focus to my work.

A very special thanks to friend and artist Joli Johnson of Hidden Akers Studio for guiding me and encouraging my ideas in the design and layout process. With her help I was able to create a vision of my stories that brings my world to life.

There's no way that I could write these stories without the help of those who came before and pioneered this place of my home. The wanderers, the trappers, miners and finally the homesteaders all had a story to tell. Gene and Ruthie Grush, the Ed Homes family to just to name a few of those who welcomed us and shared their stories.

May the stories live on.

Contents

Prologue

"The C.B. screams, 'Deadman's curve, coming down loaded.'

With maybe a hundred-fifty log trucks a day coming down the narrow Yaak road, its best to just get the hell out of the way." Four Bars and One Very White Church captures the feel and frenzy of the nineteen seventies logging mayhem in the Yaak.

My series of short stories is about the early wanderers of this place I call home. From the early 1800s to present day, the early miners and trappers who wandered into this one-of-a-kind place and the homesteaders who struggled to survive in this remote and forgotten corner of Montana had stories to tell.

The stories are of the people, and of course the wildlife, that inhabit this amazing land. Tales of creatures that are all part of this place of wonder. A place of towering trees and flowing waters carrying the river music of the wilderness.

In the story DJ, I will introduce you to a grizzly bear named DJ. "In her 21 years of wandering the wilds of the Yaak, she produced four generations with maternal lines to 58 known bears."

An injured caribou, healed by an early homestead family with love and compassion, starts the family on an amazing life they could never imaged, in The Christmas Healing.

The Yaak is changing.

In Chapters, you will meet a present day rancher, Kathryn the Third and her daughters Elizabeth Starr and Aspen Rose who come from a long line of early Yaak homesteaders.

In The Potluck, "Local developers want to increase tourism in the hopes of a big land sale. Dreams of vacation rentals cabins along the river. Tourists are replacing loggers. Log trucks have given way to recreational vehicles. Numerous environmental groups each want to be the savior of the Yaak, their latest place of 'special concern.'"

These are just a few of the issues that Kathryn and her daughters are dealing with in this rapidly changing world they call home. Their lives tell stories that bring Montana's Forgotten Corner to life.

Edd Kuropat

TALES FROM THE YAAK

PART ONE

Living on the Arrow

Is it Yaak or Yahk or Yak or maybe A'ak?

"Yaak? What's a Yaak?" Ask the tourist from Georgia as I hang paintings in my art booth.

"It's the place where I live," I respond with a smile.

"Sounds like the noise you make trying to clear your throat," her friend says.

We laugh.

When you sit in your art booth for 10 hours a day with a sign over your head reading Yaak River Originals, it stimulates questions.

Where's the Yaak? Is it in Montana? What is the Yaak? Are there Yaks in the Yaak? Do people live there?

That's just a sample of questions I find entertaining.

The Yaak is more unique than just its name. We are so far from most places that many Montanans don't know where it is, let alone that it's even in Montana.

It's a Pacific Northwest Forest which is rare in Montana, with more wildlife than people. Plenty of bears. At one time, caribou lived there.

Located next to Idaho and Washington, the Yaak is more a province of those states than Montana. We get little Montana news. The airways are owned by Spokane media and a lot of property in the Yaak is owned by people from Spokane and Coeur d'Alene, only two-and-a-half hours away. Idaho families have been gathering firewood and huckleberries in the Yaak for generations.

But where does the name Yaak come from? The Kootenay Indians who lived here named the river the Yaak, or Yahk, or A'ak or even Yac.

The Yahk river starts in southern British Columbia on Yahk Mountain. When it crosses the border, it becomes the North Fork of the Yaak River where it is joined by the East Fork, West Fork, and the South Fork to become the Yaak River which flows through the Yaak Valley. No Canadian Yahk here.

The name means the arrow on a bow. In this case, the bow is the bend of a river called the Kootenai.

The Kootenai River comes south out of Canada for 60 miles, turns West for 60 miles into Idaho then back north to Canada. It really does look like a bow. Without planes or satellites, how did Native people know that?

The Yaak/Arrow is loaded in the bow and ready to shoot towards Idaho.

Let us not forget the Canadian Yahk. On the day of friendship, American and Canadian neighbors compete in an annual baseball game. Yaak on Yahk. Beers count more than runs. Good times with good neighbors.

The name Yaak evokes fond memories. Stories of that first camp out. The first fish caught with Grandpa. Picking huckleberries with Grandma. Family hunting camps. Summers working for the Forest Service.

Yes, the Yaak is in Montana. Yes, there have been Yaks in the

Yaak. Yes, people live in the Yaak.

My favorite comment of all is from Montanans who know.

"Do you live in the Yaak?" An older gentleman asks me.

"Yes, I do."

"You live at God's County, ya know."

Yes, I know.

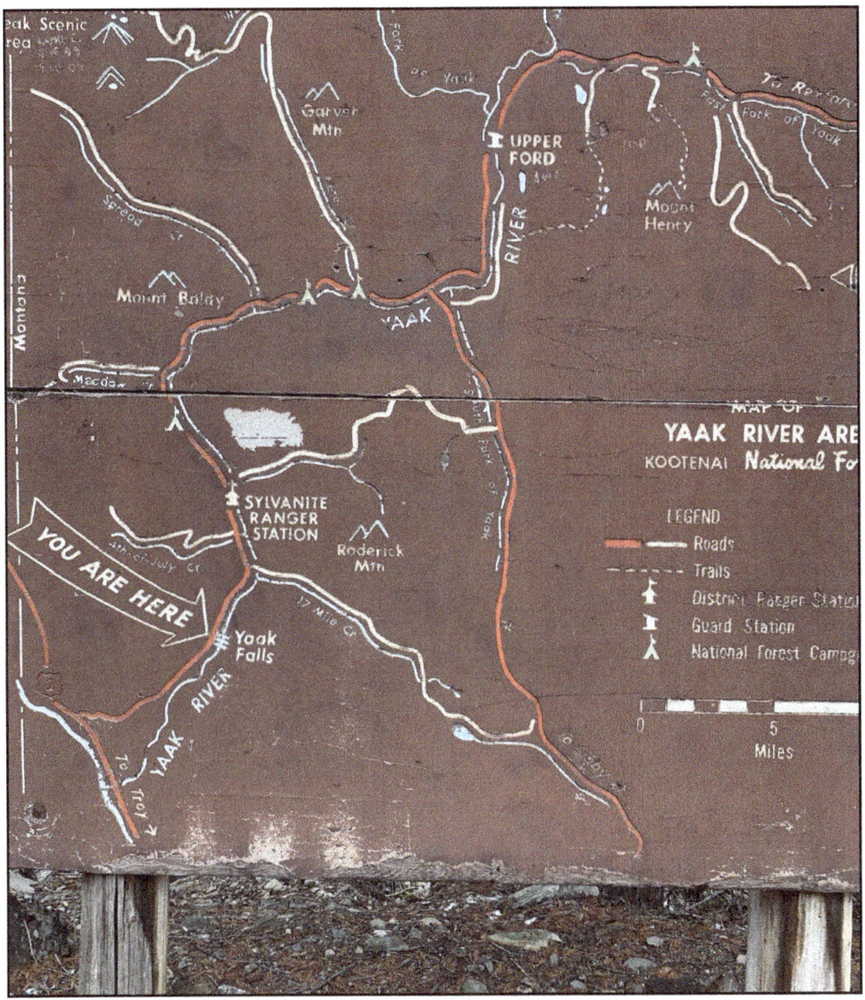

This map of the Yaak still stands beside the Yaak Falls on the Yaak River. If you are standing looking at this sign, you have officially make it to "The Yaak."

PART ONE

The Land

Whack!

Whack!

Whack!

Three corners set. One to go.

In 1862, the Homestead Act was enacted.

The Act of 1862 gave people the right to claim 160 acres of land. All you had to do was "prove" the land and pay an $18.00 filing fee. Free, if you were a Civil War Veteran. This Act created the west we live in today.

Early miners and prospectors who came to the Yaak weren't much interested in homesteading.

They were chasing that shiny metal.

Because of its remoteness, homesteading in the Yaak didn't really start until after the 1910 fire.

In the Yaak, there are 174 registered land grants and 144 are homestead grants. Most have been subdivided into smaller pieces.

Early homesteaders left their mark we see every day.

George Arbo 1896. Arbo Mountain.

Mattie Roderick 1916. Roderick Mountain.

Anton Obermeyer 1922. Obermeyer Lake.

James Hensley 1907. Hensley Hill.

Billy Hoskin 1913. Hoskin Lake.

The cornerstone of the property I live on now has 1910 carved on it from the original homestead.

Life in the Yaak has always been tough and homesteading was not easy. There was endless water, stones for a foundation, and timber for a cabin. Lacking was plentiful food. Early miners had killed off most wildlife and long deep snowy winters made food hard to grow.

Many early homesteads failed and were reclaimed by the government. Sometimes the only indication that someone once tried to build a life there are old apple trees in odd places.

Those who survived made it by working with what they had. With abundant water and many small lakes, some folks started fish hatcheries to supply small towns starting to grow.

With its giant timber, others started the first wood mills called cant mills. They would haul their mills to the timber and cut 6"x 6" cants to be used as railroad ties or to the mines in Butte to use for supports.

All early Yaak homesteaders are special but two people stand out.

In 1930, two rising stars in Hollywood decided to load a truck with supplies and head up the dirt road over Dodge Summit and down into the upper East Fork of the Yaak River. Here they found what they wanted, an abandoned homestead to claim. Paradise and privacy at last. Even for the Yaak, this was as remote as it gets. For six months every year, their home was a log cabin with no electricity or plumbing. A refuge from the limelight of Hollywood. They followed this pattern for the rest of their lives.

Their names were John McIntire and Jeanette Nolan. Wagon Train, Gunsmoke, The Virginian were a few of the many TV shows and movies they starred in.

Hollywood actors, Yaak homesteaders, and wilderness advocates, John and Jeanette proposed the first wilderness protection for the Yaak. In the mid-1970s, while others were moving into the Yaak, they were creating the 21,000-acre Mount Henry Wilderness Study Area. The first maps I got from the Forest Service showed those boundaries.

They gave presentations to local communities to try raise support. In towns where logging was the main livelihood, this wasn't an easy task. During the Wilderness Bill hearings in the 1970s, they went to Washington D.C. to present their case before Congress. Their love and passion for the Yaak was strong but, in the end, not enough. The Mount Henry Wilderness was not included in the bill and was soon forgotten.

If the Yaak ever gets its own little wilderness designation, maybe they could name it after two Yaak pioneers, John McIntire and Jeannette Nolan.

What is it that makes cant mill owners and Hollywood stars want to create a life in a remote area like the Yaak.

We who live here share many of the same answers.

The Yaak is about being. It's about wanting to be here. It's about being in the winter solitude of a snowy day. It's about being in the warmth of summertime fishing the Yaak River. It's just about being here. Pretty simple really.

Whack!

The last corner is set. Starting in 1862, the Homestead Act gave people hope that for the first time in their lives they might have a future. For the first time, they became part of a bigger picture. For the first time, they owned 160 acres of Yaak wilderness with a lot of work ahead but also the freedom to grow.

Until the Homestead Act was repealed by an act of Congress in 1976, it offered a dream for the adventurous pioneer to live on a Yaak homestead.

PART ONE

Winter's Madness

In the spring of 1978 when we moved to the Yaak Valley, some of the first people we met were Gene and Ruthie Grush. Gene and Ruthie were truly homesteaders in the Yaak.

Gene was a small man in stature but huge in life.

He'd arrived from back east in 1910 when he was only sixteen to work in fire camps that year. He saved his earnings and bought up burned-over homesteads. Gene once owned the place I live now. Rancher, logger, miner, husband, father, and owner of the only gas pump in the Yaak.

Although Gene and Ruthie lived a full homestead life, they were the first to get electricity in the valley and how Ruthie did love her electric cook stove and blender.

Gene was among the first Forest Service Rangers of the Yaak and blazed many trails that we now use as roads. He was one of few humans to ever visit the caribou calving grounds of the Yaak.

The gas pump was really the story. In its day, a very long time ago, it was high tech. The price per gallon only went up to 99 cents. You told Gene how many gallons you pumped. He took out his old cigar box, full of paperwork and change, and figured out the price.

Since Gene didn't see many people, getting gas could take a bit of time. You had to share a cup a coffee, maybe enjoy a Ruthie cookie, the latest gossip.

And you could never get away without hearing a story. Gene was a great teller of tales, smiling through his wrinkles with a sparkle in his eyes.

The serene and desolate view of the Yaak River in winter.

My favorite story concerned one winter when Ruthie kept killing herself out behind the barn.

Winter in our neck of the woods can be tough and seem never-ending. Deep snow, unrelenting cold, lack of social contact. After a while, some people go a bit wacky. Little things upset them; the dog loves you more than me kind of wacky.

Ruthie was having one of those winters.

Sure enough, one evening, something set Ruthie off, and she'd had enough. Couldn't take it anymore. Put on her bathrobe, slippers, grabbed the shotgun off the rack, and headed out the door.

"Gonna end it," she said as she disappeared into that night. Gene waited a few seconds then followed her out behind the barn to see what was up. He watched as Ruthie pointed the gun in the air and fired it. Gene calmly led her back inside.

This happened a few more times and Gene figured he better put a stop to it before something went wrong.

So he hatched a plan.

A few nights later, the cat gives Ruthie the stink eye and that's it. Bathrobe, slippers, shotgun off the rack, and out the door.

This time Gene followed quietly behind her. Ruthie pointed the gun in the air, closed her eyes, fired it off.

When she opened her eyes, Gene was standing there, covered in ketchup.

He said, "Where there's gunfire, there's blood."

And then he chuckled and looked at me with that sparkle in his eyes.

"What the heck?" I asked. "What happened next? She didn't shoot you because you're still here."

He just laughed over his success, pulling off the greatest prank ever.

Gene and Ruthie lived a long and loving life together in this place we call home.

Whenever I pick up a ketchup bottle, I must admit I still get a chuckle.

PART ONE

The First Fisherman

"The whiskey is on me, boys! "Old Jacob shouted as he laid the last of his Silver\Gold on the bar.

Old Jacob was reeling from the death a few days ago of his long-time friend and mining partner Livermore, Liver to his friends, drowned in the Yaak River. Miners and prospectors gathered at the Nugget Saloon to honor their friend and for free whiskey.

Livermore and Jacob had been partners for as long as anyone could remember. They were bonded by survival and friendship from struggling together in the wilds of the Yaak.

They met as young men, one blue, one gray, at the end of a bad war. Survivors but alone.

Gold had been discovered in this beautiful valley in Montana.

The killing was done so a deal was made. Two together was better than one alone.

Jacob claimed he did the work while Liver went fishing. Livermore didn't agree, but he liked his partner and admitted he liked to fish. As miners, they wandered many streams and creeks that bless the Yaak, searching for that elusive dream.

They were among the first prospectors in this part of wild Montana, and they liked it that way. Game was plentiful and Liver fished rivers that had never before been fished, harvesting a steady stream of Cutthroat, Bull Trout, and Redbands.

At the time, gold was being found all over Montana and the Yaak was no different. In the Yaak, gold was not normal gold but a mix of the two metals. Silver-Gold the miners called it.

Jacob and Liver spent winters in a ramshackle cabin up Fourth of July Creek, living off their summer's grubstake, waiting for spring thaw. They wanted to get back to work at their claim up Dutch Creek, but it had started to pan out.

Times were changing. Civilization came from all over the west, lured by silver-gold found around the creeks of the lower Yaak River. Claims named Independent, Keystone, Gold-flint, and Great Northern.

The Golden Nugget mine was up and running. The Nugget Saloon soon followed with its Katy Cribs of perfumed women. Saloons always popped up as the first businesses established in mining camps. Gossip circulated about starting a real town. Sylvanite they'd call it. Maybe even get a post office.

Come spring, the partners planned to move upriver and look for new ground to claim. They considered the East Fork of the Yaak but Solo Joe, who lived and trapped up that way, wasn't too fond of neighbors.

Spring couldn't come soon enough for Livermore. Not the search for gold but for fish. Liver dreamed of the sweet time in spring when the Yaak River started to clear up from spring runoff and dropped a little. And fish started to bite.

Early one morning in 1895, Livermore set out, thinking about trout for breakfast. Sad to say, he never ate that breakfast.

A short time later, miners found his body in an eddy on the river. They said he still had his rod in his hand and a fish on the hook.

He was old with shaky legs and apparently slipped on wet rocks, hit his head, and drowned. He died doing what he loved, early morning casting on a river.

Livermore was known as the first of many firsts. One of the first to come into the Yaak. One of the first to be buried in the new cemetery in the new town of Sylvanite. And, most important, the first known fisherman of the Yaak.

Another fisherman who drowned in 1910 was among the last to be buried in that cemetery.

The 1910 fire wiped out the mines and the mining town of Sylvanite. They never recovered.

The name on Livermore's grave was misspelled Liverpool. It is still at the old town site that became the Sylvanite Ranger Station.

PART ONE

The Last Cast

As that early morning light splinters through the ancient old growth timber along the Yaak River, I find myself standing in the morning river fog at fishing hole number four and contemplating a serious thought. The fish have all taken the morning off. And really, that's ok. But I cannot stop casting. You just never know what might happen.

Too be honest, it's more than just the fish part of things. It's just about being there. It's about casting into the unknown.

I am a morning fisherman and now is that special morning time. Sunlight filtering through the fog rising off the Yaak River. The constant change of reflective light swimming on the surface movements of the water.

Often the Blue Heron and I share hole number one. He gives me a look: What the heck are you doing up at this hour and in my space? We're both creatures of the morning, so he lets me stay.

No strikes but must keep casting.

At river hole number two, I watch the family of Mergansers sitting on a cedar log as I cast one line after another. After a family discussion, they decide to leave me and move down river.

Fish are rising but not for me. A few more casts to be sure.

A young whitetail mom and her fawn greet me at hole number three, but I hold off casting. We enjoy the moment of friendship, of wonderment, of sharing this river called the Yaak. It's why we're both here in early morning contentment.

I live just minutes from the Yaak River. Being an early morning riser, I start my day with a thermos of coffee, an egg sandwich, and ants in my pants. Early morning river casting sets the rhythm of the day and my world, waiting for the unknown which every sunrise brings to all of us.

Edd, flyfishing the Yaak River in June.

Rivers are the ultimate mystery. They tease you with the unknown of what's below. Rivers make you dream of what could be. Trout for breakfast maybe.

Hole number four gives two strikes on a brown floater but no fish. Strikes lead to more casting. Just never know which will be the hit.

One more cast.

Then maybe one more.

Well, maybe one more.

The thrill of the river's unknown is always strong.

Maybe cast a little to the right.

Or to the left.

Overhead the screeches of young osprey learning to fly shakes me from my river trance. The river is not just mine but a lifeline to many.

As the morning sun crest the tops of the ancient ones along the river, I realize it's time for that last cast.

One final cast. You never know.

Well, maybe one more.

The studio is calling, chores are calling, and second breakfast is calling.

Then I understand this is really not the last cast, but just a pause until the next sunrise.

El Oso Pardo

BOOM!

The shotgun was very old and had traveled far. First it belonged to his grandfather, then his father. Now it was his.

Carlito fired into the dark again.

BOOM!

"El Oso Pardo is back," he murmured. Demonio negro--the dark demon-- had already taken one of his flock.

"Follar en El Oso Pardo," he yelled into the night. Frigging grizzly bear.

Carlito was a shepherd from a family of shepherds. His grandfather, his father, and now him. He grew up watching the sheep of his Basque homeland.

He had traveled far to find himself under Montana stars on Newton Mountain in Montana's Yaak country. And he still carried his grandfather's shotgun.

One day, a man from America had showed up in his mountain village with an offer of dreams. A trip to America to shepherd his sheep in Idaho. Basque sheep headers were in demand in America.

From the Eastern Sierra to the mountains of Montana. A chance for a new life in America.

"BOOM!"

Carlito yelled, "You will not eat my children tonight, demonio negro!"

Sheep corrals on Newton Mountain are still there today.

After the 1910 fires decimated the Yaak and Western Montana, grass grew back first. And lots of it. Abundant grass didn't go unnoticed by big sheep operations in southern Idaho and eastern Washington. At one point, an estimated 35,000 sheep grazed on the burned-over hills of western Montana, including the Yaak.

Good for sheep. Not so good for grizzly bears. Historical data says, in the Bitterroot Mountains alone during this time, up to 40 grizzlies were killed annually.

In the year nineteen fourteen, Carlito and his flock had arrived at the train depot in Moyie Springs. From there, he worked his sheep through the meadows of Pine Creek, Ferrell Creek, onto the slopes of Tepee Mountain, and eventually to the Newton Mountain ridge. Here, he spent his summer grazing his flock through the high basins and meadows.

He was not alone.

In his homeland, he had dealt with many predators. He knew about wolves and coyotes and the occasional small bear.

But grizzly bears, never. That's what the sheep owners called them.

El Oso Pardo to Carlito. They told him to kill every one he saw. They gave him lots of shotshells.

That was not who he was. He was a shepherd, not a killer. He was a shepherd because he loved wandering the natural world and all it brought him. As a shepherd, he watched. He watched the amazing creatures of this wild land they called El Yak. He watched the sunrises and sunsets over his Montana mountain ridge. At night, he loved watching the amazing Yaak stars.

His days were busy hauling water from a spring he found just off the ridge. He built circular stone corrals to hold the sheep at night. When the sheep owners came with supplies, they always asked how many Osos he had killed. He would just mumble, "Many."

"Good," they said.

"BOOM!" Another blast into the dark from the old gun.

Carlito was not a killer, but he had to protect his flock. He already lost a sheep, and this bothered him deeply.

El Oso Pardo was the devil, he told himself. Even his sheepdogs were afraid of this one. He had seen him at a great distance. Big and black with a large hump going grey.

When Carlito first saw him, he couldn't imagine him as a killer. The huge bear was rolling around in a berry patch, eating berries and sleeping.

But a killer, he was. El Oso Pardo had taken one of his children and Carlito swore he would take no more.

***

Demonio negro was hungry. It seemed he was always hungry now. He was a survivor. As a young cub, he had somehow lived through the great burning. He survived by feeding on the carcasses of those that did not.

Those first years were not easy for the few survivors. Food was scarce, found only in small areas that did not burn. Roaming the valleys and mountains of the Yaak, he avoided the man camps and growing homesteads. He learned about barking dogs there and did not like them. He found food in other places and grew into the strong, beautiful grizzly he was.

El Oso Pardo could not see well in the dark, but he smelled them and the man. It had been easy to take the first one. But no longer. Stone walls protected them. The man's shouts and the booming agitated him.

BOOM! "Not tonight, demonio negro!" The man shouted again.

Demonio negro decided this wasn't the time and worked his way back down to the river valley and easier pickings.

***

The rest of that summer, Carlito had no more trouble from his demonio negro. When he saw other grizzlies, a simple blast in the air from his shotgun sent them running.

In late summer, it was time to work the flock down to the Moyie River and onto the railroad in Moyie Springs.

Someday, Carlito would tell his grandchildren the story of his battle to save his flock from the Great Montana demonio negro. He wasn't sure if he would tell them he never aimed at El Oso Pardo but only into the sky.

***

Thankfully, in the late 1930s, the Forest Service ended large-scale sheep grazing on timber lands.

But the damage from sheep grazing in western Montana had been done. Many hillsides were overgrazed. Grizzlies had been shot on sight. Wildlife habitats took years to recover.

Now, when I hike or fish or ski the ridge of Newton Mountain, sometimes I eat lunch sitting on the old stone corrals that remain. I try to imagine the Yaak in Carlito's day--no timber, hillsides of barren stubble, devoid of wildlife.

This place called the Yaak is a survivor, like the creatures it protects. A survivor of fire, flooding, overgrazing, greedy timber companies, passions of protectionists.

Through it all, this land survives.

PART ONE

Charlie's Waterfall

Old knees. Old hands. Old bones.

Maybe that's why they called him Old Charlie.

Just another worn-out old prospector, Charlie was.

But a proud prospector he was, by God.

Not a cave-dwelling miner, by God.

Many years before, a young, strong child of the Great Plains made his way to the Yaak. Charlie had been infected by the fever.

The fever for gold in them thar hills.

When he got off the train in Troy, he started walking up the Yaak River trail to the mining town of Sylvanite. After the dry winds and blazing plains where he'd come from, he could not believe a place like this existed. He had never seen so much flowing water, rivers and creeks everywhere he looked. The trees were taller than the tallest buildings and so thick they blocked out the sun.

Charlie had found his own heaven and would never leave this place called the Yaak.

He easily got a job when a new mine opened but quickly realized working underground wasn't for him. The mining town of

Sylvanite wasn't for him. Drunk miners, scheming mine owners, and the whole Wild West thing wasn't for him.

He bided his time and saved his wages until he put his grubstake together.

Then, he set out to prospect his new world and never looked back. While some saw nothing but wilderness, Charlie saw home. For the rest of his life, he wandered the many streams and forks of the Yaak River. He became friends with fellow prospectors. Scattered homesteaders gave him winter shelter and food.

Charlie was a loner and he liked it that way. Used to say that whenever miners try to work together and something goes wrong, they look for someone to blame. Working alone, he only had himself to blame.

Charlie was old now. Everything hurt on his body, and he knew his time was coming to an end. He hated going into Sylvanite to resupply his grubstake. The miners kidded him about his old clothes, his old tools, and his old looks.

But the miners needed prospectors because Old Charlie and those like him found gold. Then the mines followed with good jobs.

Whenever Charlie came to town, miners took him to the saloon and got him drunk on whiskey like they were old friends. Then they'd try to get him to talk about his latest finds.

Charlie played the game well. He drank their whiskey and told a tale or two but never said where or what he found. That angered the miners. They cursed him and called him a worthless old prospector who would never find a flake of gold.

This trip, Charlie knew he wasn't going to leave the town. He was tired. And sick. And old.

But not sad. He took comfort in the life he'd lived in the Yaak, knowing it had been more than he'd ever hoped for as a young man. He lived his life well and to its fullest.

Now he was tired.

The town had just put in a new cemetery along the Yaak River, and Charlie would be pleased to spend eternity there among the wildflowers.

But he had one more tale to tell before he met his maker.

That morning he was pleased that he'd awakened for one more day. He moved slowly and didn't feel well. He gathered his meager belongings, went to the little white church in town, and asked the preacher to give them to whoever might need them. He also gave the preacher a little sack of gold for the church and a letter to be opened one month after his death.

Then he took his last slow walk to the Nugget Saloon where he made his way to the bar. As the barkeep watched, Old Charlie pulled out a weathered pouch and slowly emptied its contents on the bar.

A sudden quiet fell over the bar like never before.

Lying on the bar next to the pouch were some of the biggest gold nuggets ever seen in the Yaak.

"Give me a bottle of your best whiskey," Charlie said. "The imported stuff."

As the crowd gathered to admire his gold and get free whiskey, questions flew.

They asked where he'd found the gold.

"Burnt Creek?"

"Fourth of July Creek?"

"Maybe Seventeen Mile Creek?"

Charlie drank down a shot of the best whiskey he'd ever had. Then he said, "Boys, found the mother lode. But to be honest, my days are numbered. I'll tell ya the truth. It's at the bottom of that waterfall on..."

With those last words, Old Charlie fell over and kicked the spittoon bucket dead.

The crowd was stunned, shocked, and more than a little pissed.

"What waterfall?"

"Which creek?"

"Wake up, Charlie!" they screamed.

But Charlie was gone. Literally kicked the bucket.

If there's one thing miners like to do besides mine, it's argue. And argue they did. Each had his own sure and certain opinion as to what Old Charlie's last words had been.

Pete Creek, some said.

Some said, Hellroaring Creek, maybe.

Must be upriver, others said.

Can't be Yaak Falls, Charlie never panned there. On that fact, they agreed.

I am not saying if this waterfall... Spread Creek Falls, is Charlie's Waterfall. Maybe it is. Maybe it isn't.

Soon the waterfall scramble began in earnest.

If you want to find a waterfall in the Yaak, just walk up the creek, right?

Not as easy as it sounds.

Round, shiny, slippery Rocky Mountain river rocks make up the streams.

Many sprained ankles and twisted knees resulted.

Many a miner got soaked, but they found waterfalls. Some with altars behind them. Some with pools too deep to pan. Some with dead cutthroats that could journey no farther.

The upper Yaak homesteaders heard Charlie's story. Since he'd spent lots of time in their area, they started their own search. They panned falls on Turner Creek and the cascading falls on the West Fork. All to no avail.

Miners and homesteaders floundered up many Yaak creeks. For years to come, they told the story of the gold that was never found under the waterfall.

Even after the truth came out, some still searched.

A month after Charlie's passing, the town preacher read the note Charlie had left. Charlie knew the greed of miners and wanted to play a joke on them.

The gold he'd placed on the bar came from a lifetime of Yaak prospecting. There had never been one big strike.

The satisfaction of his life was never about the shining metal. It was sleeping under the Montana wilderness stars. The food and shelter this land provided him. The freedom the Yaak gave him to be himself.

As a prospector, he loved messing with the miners. And, thanks to him, they were all wet.

Charlie was buried with a grin on his face in the new Sylvanite Cemetery next to a recently deceased fisherman who'd been in on the joke.

***

The Yaak is blessed with many things. At the top of the list are its abundance of flowing waters. From small cascades to vertical falls, water makes everything work here, with some of the highest concentration of waterfalls and cascades anywhere in Montana. The Upper West Fork falls serve to keep the last genetically pure Redband trout safe from other fish.

I have taken many visitors to falls in the Yaak. A couple of sprained ankles and a twisted knee are the souvenirs. Still, the treks are worth it because there are waterfalls yet to be found.

And maybe even Old Charlie's gold.

PART ONE

Sourdough Gone Bad

Whack! The bullet hits the tamarack Buddy the Sheriff is hiding behind.

"Damn it, Olson," Buddy yells, "that was too close. Quit shooting at me. We just want to help you."

Whack! Another bullet says hi farther up in the western larch.

"I don't need no help," Olson yells back from inside his cabin. "Just leave me be."

"You know I can't do that, Olson," Buddy shouts. "You done hurt those boys and killed one of them and that isn't right."

Whack! Another bullet hits the tree. Right now, Buddy loves this old tamarack. He guesses it's thirty inches on the butt, good solid cover.

"Didn't mean to kill them, just wanted to make them sick so they would leave me be." Olson adds, "Don't like all this new government happenings, at all."

"Too late to let things be, Olson. You killed someone and there's a price to pay for that. That's for the judge to decide, not us." Buddy tries to inject hopefulness in his voice. "We're here to help you, not shoot you. But you gotta understand, we're not leaving without you."

As Buddy hunkers down, admiring his beautiful protective tree, he wonders why he didn't listen a month ago when old Solo Joe complained about Olson. Maybe a boy would still be alive today.

Solo Joe Perrault was a French fur trapper, miner, prospector, and wanderer of his upper Yaak world, living alone for over 25 years. From his cabin at the East Fork of the Yaak to Dodge Summit, he trapped and searched for that elusive gold sparkle.

He had one neighbor within 10 miles. Olson.

The month before, Solo Joe had come to town to sell some gold, buy his grubstake, and drink a little whiskey. And talk to the sheriff about his neighbor Olson who was going "dingle on the bean." Dangerously crazy. Olson had set bear traps around Solo Joe's claim, hoping Joe would get caught in one.

"Son of a bitch is going to hurt someone, and he says it's probably me." Joe added, "If you see him, just pretend he's a grizzly bear and shoot him, would you?"

Buddy had shaken his head. "Can't really arrest someone just because their neighbors think they're crazy. Most of the people in this country could be called crazy just for being here."

If only Buddy had listened, a homestead family wouldn't be having a funeral.

Solo Joe's words soon came true.

The new Forest Service Ranger of the new Yaak Forest District told Buddy that he'd hired a couple of local homesteaders to start cutting a trail from the East Fork up to Dodge Summit and down to the Kootenai River. Apparently, those two upset Olson by cutting trail near his place. He shouted threats at them. One day they got back to their cabin and found Olson lurking around. He claimed he just wanted to say hi.

Next morning the boys were just finishing up their sourdough flapjacks when they started to get sick. One boy had eaten a lot. He quickly died. The other, who had eaten less, realized something was wrong and bolted down the trail to Solo Joe's place. Joe was able to help him.

The Ranger reported, "Somebody poisoned my boys, and we need to find him and arrest him."

Messing with a person's sourdough flapjacks is as low as it gets. "We'll find him," Buddy said.

The trip into the wilderness had been tough. The country doctor came along to verify the death and figure out what killed him. They'd loaded up the horses on the train to Troy where they met the Ranger. The Yaak was now Forest Service land which made it his land.

From there, a slow ride to the mining town of Sylvanite then to the junction with the South Fork of the Yaak. They spent the night at Maddie Roderick's place, then up to the North Fork where they met the homesteaders who'd lost a son and gave their condolences. The doctor had hoped to examine the body, but he was already buried.

After more hard miles, they arrived at Solo Joe's place. Solo said he'd guide them to the line cabin where the boys got poisoned, but no closer. "Don't want my leg ending up in a grizzly trap."

When they got to the camp, the doc only needed one sniff of the sourdough to figure it out.

"Arsenic" he said, "smells like almond. Son of gun poisoned their flapjacks."

***

For the past hour, Buddy has stared up at the big tree. No bullets for a while. He's had enough.

"Ok, Olson," Buddy calls, "I'm tired, hungry, and starting to get pissed you shooting at me. Come out or I will burn your ass out."

The end is anticlimactic. Olson ran out of bullets and really needed to take a piss. He walks out of his cabin and asks them not to shoot him while he's peeing. They don't.

Buddy makes sure the Ranger makes the arrest. It's his land. They were his boys. It could be the first arrest done by the new Ranger in this new Forest Service.

The trip home is slow. They stop at the homestead family's place and make Olson apologize for taking their son.

When it is all said and done, Olson is ruled insane and sent to the new mental hospital in Warm Springs.

Some think Solo Joe Perrault was crazy and lonely. How wrong they are. He left the busy streets of France to escape into the wilderness of Montana where he discovered his vibe in the nature of the Yaak. He found the comfort he had traveled so far to find.

Solo Joe lived out his life in the Yaak he loved, in that harmony of the soul that only comes from nature's vibe.

The Yaak simply touches your soul and will not let go. Solo Joe felt this touch. So do the few that live here.

Sadly, that touch was not enough to rescue Olson from demons inside him. Or maybe he didn't want to share his piece of heaven with anyone else.

The trail worker who survived the poisoned flapjacks was Ed Stahl. Ed went on to build the trail over Dodge Summit and down to the ferry on the Kootenai River, pretty much single-handed. One tough dude.

One unresolved aspect of this crime still bothers me.

Keeping a sourdough starter fed and growing is a true art and a difficult skill to master. A starter that's taken care of lasts for years and is handed down through generations like an heirloom.

How could Olson stoop so low to destroy a sourdough starter?

PART ONE

DJ

DJ was the single child of a single mom, the result of a one-night stand. The home birth took place in a remote area of the Yaak. For the rest of her life, she would know no other world than wilderness.

She spent her early days like any mountain child, playing in flower-covered meadows along the Yaak River, swimming in the summer in the high mountain Wee Lake, trying but failing to catch fish. Mom was always on watch, keeping her safe.

With an abundance of food, DJ grew quickly. When she discovered her first fall huckleberries, she fell in love. If she could, she would eat berries dawn till dusk.

Exploring her world was a daily education, with her young days full of discoveries. Mom raised her child well, keeping her close, teaching her to avoid strangers because the wilderness held dangers all around.

As days became shorter and nights colder, Mom encouraged DJ to eat as much as possible to create winter fat. After exploring the area, they returned to their winter homestead and settled in for a cozy winter. DJ's first year was a good one. Her next summer was a copy of the first.

In her third year, when spring arrived in their world, they emerged from their winter home.

Now life was different. This would be their last time together as mother and daughter. The child had grown, and both knew it was time for DJ to make her own way.

That spring, a new smell drifted in the air that they had never experienced before.

They smelled humanity and all it brought, progress with machines, human cooking aromas, and the smell of fear. Humans feared the wilderness and the unknown that was DJ's world.

The mountains behind my home became her home, filled with lakes and flower-covered meadows. We later determined she'd been born about the same time we arrived the Yaak. Together, yet apart, we each explored the surrounding wilderness.

She was a shy, secretive neighbor. Never came to potlucks or Easter parties. Never shared a glass of moonshine. Yet she became the one closest to my heart.

To those who got to know her, she would serve as a beacon of hope.

We never met face to face but one day she introduced herself. I came home to find a GIANT Bear poop right at my front door. Her way of saying hello?

Home births were common in the Yaak. One summer day, a baby was born in the valley and the afterbirth was placed in a shed for burial the next day. That night, a bear broke in and carried it away. Grizzly tracks were found. Was this her omen to let us know she was the valley matron?

This was a time of change in the Yaak and not for the better. Fear of wilderness was strong. All things wild were hated and killed if possible. Funny how humans are taught to hate something before we are taught to understand it.

At one point in a grizzly's life, a person only had to pay 100 pennies for a tag to kill her. Paintings showed her kind attacking homesteaders and livestock.

No one ever painted a picture of her rolling in a huckleberry patch.

She had never caused harm in her life, but she was at the top of the hate list.

Meadows turned into farms. Houses were built in the wilderness.

DJ survived in the only way she knew, by learning. She avoided all humanity and their smells. High mountain lakes and meadows became the sanctuary where she thrived.

Even though her kind were becoming fewer, she found a mate for occasional one-night stands. She started a family of her own. Her mother had taught her well and she passed on those teachings to her own children.

In the spring of 1986, she met humans up close for the first time.

Even though she wasn't a black bear, she was caught in a black bear study trap.

Her official name became Female Grizzly 106 but her nickname was DJ.

This is the oldest Grizzly ever trapped in the Cabinet Mountains, estimated to be around 30 years of age.

She met biologist Wayne Kasworm and the grizzly study group that followed her amazing story for the next 13 years.

As of 2014, Wayne and his group estimated DJ began the maternal line of all current female grizzlies in the Yaak, with up to 28 offspring between the British Columbia Yahk and the Montana Yaak. With new DNA testing they determined that, in her 21 years of wandering the wilds, she produced four generations with matrilines to 58 known bears. In 2018, one daughter, seven granddaughters, and five great-granddaughters were detected roaming in the Yaak.

All from a single mom.

This story became personal because DJ and her cubs were killed in the wilderness behind my home.

In the spring of 2019, the study group noticed DJ's collar hadn't moved from her winter den. On further investigation they found that DJ had been dug out of her den, killed, and eaten. She died defending her cubs who were also killed and consumed. Conspecific they called it, indicating another grizzly was responsible for the deaths and consumption.

The wilderness isn't always kind.

Wayne Kasworm had developed such respect for DJ and her story that he posted her obituary in the local paper.

While DJ's brutal death is sad, it is a natural event in the cycle of life in the wilderness. When her kind came under threat of extinction, she ensured their survival. She taught lessons of immeasurable understanding into the world of the grizzly.

She was a quiet neighbor, a good mother, grandmother, great grandmother.

She was the wild in my wilderness.

Special thanks to Wayne Kasworm and those other Grizzly Guardians for the technical information and for what they do.

PART ONE

Old Bones

One step.

Two steps.

Then another step. Then another. Don't stop moving, the trapper told himself. You stop, you die. One step after another.

The day had not gone according to plan. What was supposed to be a simple snowshoe up the South Fork of Meadow Creek to check his trap line had become a life and death struggle.

One more step. Keep moving. He never felt such pain before.

The blood from his wounds soaked into his clothes.

Survival in the wilderness required making somewhat smart decisions. His decision had not been smart.

What the hell was he thinking, crawling into that wolverine's den? Greed made him do it. When he found the Carcajou track leading to its den, all he could think about was how an Indian devil's hide would really help his winter grubstake. Prices were high right now.

The smell had been overwhelming, but greed pushed him forward. Crawling with pistol in hand, he'd barely entered the den chamber when it attacked.

Wolverines are known as one bad-ass animal. Strong, aggressive, fearless, smelly, and just plain mean.

The trapper never had a chance. In the narrow confines of the den, the animal shredded the trapper's hands and arms and took a big chunk of his scalp. Then, for some reason, it stopped.

With all the strength the trapper could muster, he backed out of the den. As he stood, pain overwhelmed him. His hands and arms were almost useless. Somehow, he was able to put on his snowshoes, shoulder his pack, and start moving. The blood from his scalp wounds ran down his back.

One step, then another. It was snowing harder than ever. Keep moving.

He knew he needed to get to shelter quickly, and he knew where that was. Two years past, he found a black bear den in the base of a huge cedar tree. The bears had dug out the inside of the tree for a cozy winter den. It would give him shelter while he bound his wounds. It would also give him protection from the wolverine which was probably following his blood trail. They were pure meat eaters.

At last, he spotted the massive tree and the small opening at the base. With his last strength, he removed his snowshoes, crawled inside, and was relieved to find it empty. He wedged his snowshoes to block the opening. He bound up his wounds as best he could, but the pain was unforgiving, and movement became harder and harder.

He needed to rest. Then, in the morning, try to make it back to the mining town of Sylvanite.

It was not to be. As the trapper dozed off, the blood loss and serious wounds were too much for his body to overcome. He passed in the womb of the ancient guardian tree that became his tomb.

As decades went by, the tree continued to grow. Slowly the small opening grew over and was covered in forest debris. Insects and rodents slowly consumed his clothes and flesh until all that was left was the skeleton of the trapper, entombed in a massive cedar tree.

The Yaak is home to some of the largeset old growth trees, estimated at over 200 years old.

The tree had been born before people came into its world. Time was not kind to the massive tree. While it was huge at the base, it was no longer the tallest in its grove of companions. A lighting strike took out most of the top and a micro-burst opened it to the elements. Over time, rain and snow slowly rotted the middle until it became an almost-hollow tree.

Still it grew, protecting and guarding its secret.

Into the late seventies and early eighties.

Funny how you know it's four o'clock on Friday in the Yaak just by watching the firewood boys show up in the parking lot of the Nugget Saloon, waiting for the magic hour.

One Forest Service rig after another comes home to roost at the Sylvanite Ranger Station. Other than a couple of seasonals, no Forest Service employees actually live in the Yaak.

By four thirty-five, government employees have departed and won't be back until Monday.

Then the fun begins for the boys with the pickups.

These are not your average firewood cutters. These are cedar boys. To be honest, more likely cedar poachers. And the Yaak has cedar, big old cedar perfect for making roofing shingles for the booming California market. Prices are high for cedar bolts. Now, they love that cedar roofing, but later they'll pay the real cost when wildfires scorch California.

Every place has an underground economy and the Yaak is no different. No names, no paperwork. just cash. For various reasons, timber theft on the National Forest land is almost impossible to prosecute.

This group is led by Big Louie who's not big at all. He just happens to have the biggest chainsaw. This is a serious group of men who take their work seriously. Running 090 Stihl chainsaws with 40-inch bars with chisel chains. High-powered headlamps for night work because they always work in the dark.

For some time, Big Louie has had his eyes on a massive, but short, old cedar tree up the South Fork of Meadow Creek. Big enough to fill four trucks with bolts. At least two grand maybe.

Tonight is the night.

It doesn't take long on the dirt roads for the boys to get to the old cedar. In the dark, with their headlamps, the tree looks foreboding. With its huge size and shadows dancing on its rough bark, the tree looks almost spooky.

It's too big for even long chainsaw bars so they will have to cut out pieces to make the undercut on the front.

As Big Lou goes to start his saw, a funny thing happens. Pull after pull on the starter rope and nothing. It won't start.

The crew yells, "What the hell is wrong with your saw? We don't have all night."

"Don't know," Lou says, cussing under his breath. "It was running great at home."

After much pulling, playing with the choke, and a whole lot more cussing, the saw finally starts. The idea is to cut a level cut first and then up the angle cut so they won't waste the butt wood. As Big Louie starts his cut, the chain comes off the bar and flies into his face, cutting his cheek.

"What the hell is going on?" Lou screams as he wipes blood from his cheek. "That's never happened before."

In short order, they get the chain back on, the saw starts, and the cutting begins. First the level cut, then bringing up the angle cut. A couple of small vertical cuts in the wedge. Axes try to break out the wedge. After some solid hits, it comes out in pieces.

"Son of a bitch, it's hollow," someone says. "Not gonna be much shingle wood here."

Another says, "Shine your light in there and see what you can. Maybe it's only thin in the front."

As Lou gets down and directs his light into the opening, he can't figure out what he's seeing.

After a few seconds, he realizes what he's looking at and falls backwards, stunned and freaked out.

"What the hell's wrong with you?" The crew asks.

Big Lou is barely able to speak. "There's bones in there and a skull was looking at me."

"Bullshit, you're just messing with us."

Mouth gaping, all Louie can do is point his shaking hand at the opening.

One by one, the crew takes turns shining their headlamps into the opening, putting light on the old trapper for the first time in hundred years.

WTF?

Son of a bitch.

What the hell?

This is messed up.

It's a tomb.

The last comment: This is bad karma, messing with a grave.

Little do they know that bad karma is just beginning.

The crew is freaked, and some want to get the hell out of there. Others want to take the bones.

Louie and the rest want to finish what they came for. Two grand is a lot of money to pass up.

As Lou struggles to start his saw again, a night breeze starts blowing.

Then they hear it.

A low, but steady, mournful sound coming from the tree. A sad, lonely moan.

That's all it took for a group of tough loggers to take off running and stumbling in the dark through the woods. Every monster that scared them as kids is now after them, they're sure of it.

The curse begins.

As the crew regroups at the trucks and tries to leave, two rigs have dead batteries and must be push-started. Then tires begin to flatten, two on the way to the main road.

Over the next couple of weeks, their luck goes downhill fast. Chainsaws won't start. Trucks break down. Endless flat tires.

They can't tell anyone what they found for fear the Feds will bust them.

The worst for Louie are the nightmares of the skull looking at him.

When the crew starts getting cut while using their saws, Lou knows they have to fix this somehow before someone gets killed. They hold a meeting to figure out how to make amends with a pile of bones in a tree.

One says, "Never had a proper burial, just died alone in the dark. Maybe give him a funeral."

Another of the crew came from an old upper Yaak homestead family. He says, back in the day when a person was buried, his family and friends would put small special gifts of faith and love with the departed. Something to have with them wherever they might end up.

So, they hatch a plan.

In hopes of forgiveness, each member brings something important to them to give to the bones.

Two days later, in broad daylight, they gather at the base of the ancient tree. No way they're coming back in the dark. A slight breeze is blowing, and they still hear a quiet moan.

One by one, they place their offerings into the opening. One brings a traditional parting gift of tobacco. Two bring bottles of their favorite whiskey, only the best for the bones. A couple others offer their best pipe weed from their summer harvest. One contributes fresh elk jerky.

Whiskey, elk jerky, pipe weed, and tobacco. Sounds like a party.

After the gifts are set at the base, they attempt to replace the wedge pieces as tight as they can. Each asks forgiveness from the tree and bones in their own way. They notice the moaning stops.

They return to their trucks and are relieved when the engines start and there are no flat tires on the way out.

As the days pass, their bad luck seems to be over. But never again do they poach cedar or go anywhere near the South Fork of Meadow Creek.

If you find yourself wandering among the ancient ones around here on a windy day, you just might hear the soft moan of the trapper in his sanctuary.

You see, the way Big Louie cut the undercut, with the tree partially hollow, when the wind blew, it became a giant flute and made a soft low sound.

Or maybe it's just the moan of an old trapper who wants to be left alone, wrapped in the womb-tomb of an ancient cedar tree.

PART ONE

Four Bars

Dodging logging trucks is a full-time job these days.

The CB screams, "Dead man's curve, coming downloaded."

"Better pull over, Jimmy," I say to my pal. "Sounds like South Paw."

"Yea, he doesn't give much room." Jimmy replies. He's driving his 1975 F 150, a good solid pickup but no match for a loaded logging rig.

I grab the CB mike and call out, "Pickup headed up at twenty-two miles."

It's the late 1970s and early 1980s and the Yaak is being logged like never before because of the beetle epidemic that's infested lodgepoles.

With maybe a hundred-fifty log trucks a day coming down the narrow Yaak road, it's best just to get the hell out of the way and make yourself known. You do not want to end up in the river, that's for sure.

You can't safely drive the Yaak road without a CB. The Forest Service goal seems to be cut down every last lodgepole in the forest.

Which has led to a whole lotta log trucks.

And a whole lotta loggers.

Most have names on their trucks like Mustang, Blue Hauler, or South Paw, or even Hollywood. Hollywood is the funniest. He drags it out like "coooooming doooooown looooooaded."

Most drivers are careful and courteous.

And some aren't. At the end of the day, it's all about load counts. Who has the most? These are the scary ones. The CB is busy.

Jimmy and I are heading up the Yaak road to the South Fork to work on a thinning unit contract we got. Another day of nine-by-nine tree spacing in the rain. You do what you gotta do around here.

If you live in the Yaak these days, you work in the woods. It's a forestry economy. No tourists, no building trades, no hunting lodges. It's woods work, pure and simple. From planting the trees to logging the trees and everything in between. On one side, the epidemic has created a lot of work for folks like me and Jim. On the other side of the story, the hills are being stripped bare.

I call our warning over the CB, "Pickup headed up the South Fork."

Jimmy asks, "Burritos at the Strip?"

For sure. The best part of this job is coming up the South Fork Road for burritos at the Cherokee Strip.

There are only five establishments in the Yaak: four bars and one very white church.

The bars in the Yaak are more than just drinking establishments. They're a warm community place with a roof. Potlucks, movie nights, and of course music. Family times. Jobs are found. Business deals are done. Bars are the center of all that's happening at the time.

Yaak Bar Number One is the Cherokee Strip, one of the coolest saloons anywhere, located in bum frigging nowhere on the South

The Dirty Shame Saloon is legendary in the Yaak Region. It was originally opened in the 1950's and is still in business today.

Fork Road. No power but great people and good food. A couple of pool tables and the best beer cooler anywhere. They have no power so, to keep the beer cold, they run water from the creek behind the bar into a cement trough full of beer. Way cool.

They also brought a generator and VCR player for movie nights in the Yaak. High tech!

The CB screams, "Six mile down the South Fork loaded."

"Pickup with burritos headed up," I call back.

The guy on the other end of the CB laughs.

Jimmy and I spend a long day running a chainsaw to kill a whole lot of little trees. After work, we head out back down the South Fork and stop at Yaak Bar Number Two, the Shame. It is Friday, after all.

The one and only Dirty Shame. The oldest bar in the Yaak. Started when they built the Air Force base in the upper Yaak in the '50s. The Russians were coming so the Army put cat roads zigzagging everywhere up to the Canadian border. And those tractor operators and army folks needed a beer.

You can still find those cat roads today.

Today's Friday and busy with loggers and a road crew that's paving the upper Yaak. The state says it will help bring the tourists in.

Not everyone wants a paved road. Some folks worry for the grizzlies in the area. Bars are not the best places for heated discussions. Last week, when a friend expressed his concern for the bears, he was roughed up by the road crew. This is sad because it's always been a great family bar.

Tonight, Jimmy and I are cautious. We play our Shake-a-Day, get our beers to go, and leave.

Shake-a-Day is a ritual here. It's like a western gunfight–you don't even have to say a word. Walk in, put a quarter on the bar, and nod your head. The dice cup come out and you shake. If you lose the quarter, it goes into the Shake-a-Day jug which can reach hundreds of dollars. If you win, you get a beer.

Montana law says you can legally drink and drive and get booze to go. Go cups are common. Local bars advertise what's called a Yaak Attack. Start with a drink in Libby, then a drink in Troy, then hit all four bars in the Yaak and some how make it back to Libby without dying or killing somebody.

We sit in Jimmy's rig, drinking our beers and waiting for a log truck to come along that we can follow down. Safer to follow than get in front of one.

Jimmy crumples his empty and says, "I heard they're going to start widening the Yaak road in a couple of years."

"Seeing is believing," I say.

Over the CB, a logger calls out, "Cowgirl headed up at eighteen miles, driving like a bat out of hell."

"Must be Jeanette," Jimmy says.

As in Jeanette Nolan. Yeah, that Jeanette Nolan, old-time movie and TV actress. The truckers call her cowgirl because she always wears Western outfits. And, sure enough, here she comes flying up the road in her little red car.

Eyes straight ahead, both hands on steering wheel and dodging logging trucks with determination.

Yaak Bar Number Three: The Hellroaring Saloon.

Time to get a refresher and a little pizza from two of the nicest people in the Yaak. Run by Don and Diane, a long-time valley family. Don serves and Diane cooks the pizzas. Always a fishing update to be had at the Hellroaring.

Don likes the lakes. Never trusted the river even though he lives 50 feet from it. They sponsor the Shame to Hellroaring raft race every year and he cooks a bunch of ribs and people bring potluck dishes. Really good times.

The fourth and last bar of the Yaak is the Golden Nugget, our neighborhood hangout. A fun family bar run by a great couple who are musicians. Twice a month, they host a potluck and music jam. People bring food and every kind of instrument—guitars, banjos, drums, a fiddle or two, mandolins, even a stand-up bass. Good food, good music, and good friends.

But not today. It's Friday night and the bar is full of log truck drivers and timber cutters, doing that macho thing. Shake-a-Days for six packs of open beers. If you win, you have to chug all six.

Not our crowd. Jimmy and I head home to get off the road before these people get behind the wheel.

As I call out the last mile marker, we turn off the highway 508 road and I kill the CB for the day.

"Going fishing?" Jimmy asks.

"Yep," I say. "You?"

"Yep." Jimmy responds.

"Where you headed?" I ask.

"Up to that you're-not-gonna-find-me lake. And you?"

"Probably hit those you're-not-gonna-find-me beaver ponds."

We laugh.

Jim asks, "You think if this new road that's coming will really bring in the tourists and hurt the fishing?"

"Not sure," I say. "Probably not, though. Unless someone writes a book about our little world."

"Don't forget, we live in bum frigging nowhere and who would really want to live here?"

***

By the mid '80s the Beetle mayhem ended. The logging industry collapsed. Work became scarce. The loggers moved on and it got quiet again for awhile.

The Cherokee Strip is gone now, just a chimney with a pile of ashes, but the vibe is not forgotten.

Hellroaring Saloon and the Golden Nugget no longer exist.

When I go fishing and hiking, I drive by those old haunts a lot and the memories still bring a smile of past good times and those burritos from the Strip.

On a solemn note, more than one tragedy happened on that gnarly-ass 508 road, drinking and driving, or not. Log truck drivers, fishermen, firewood cutters, locals just coming home.

The Yaak has changed. So have Montana's liquor and gambling laws. In 2005, open containers were outlawed. In towns these days, casinos are on every corner.

Saddest to say, Shake-a-Day is no longer legal.

PART ONE

Humility and Modesty

"Just kill the damn thing, will ya?" The old Forest Service forester tells the new trainee. They sit in their rig, staring at it.

"Why should I do that?" The young trainee asks, her brows crinkled.

"Because that's what we do," the old timber beast says. "What are they teaching you kids in forestry school these days? This is the real world here in the woods of the Yaak. It's our job to protect these woods."

"From that?" The greenhorn asks.

Her boss grunts. "Wasn't too long ago we could carry a pistol in our rigs to shoot the damn things, but not anymore. So just grab the shovel in the back and give it a whack, will ya?"

Earlier this week, the new forester started her career at the Sylvanite Ranger Station in the Yaak District. Even though she's confused, she figures it's best to do what her boss says. She gets out, walks around to the back of the pickup, and finds the shovel.

She rubs her gloves along the smooth handle, stalling. She really doesn't want to follow his orders but steels herself as she walks around the pickup to do the dirty deed.

Through the open truck window, the boss says, "Look at what the damn thing did to that sign. Another one that will have to be replaced."

"Why did you want to kill it?" The trainee swallows to keep the quake out of her voice. "It's so small."

The crusty Forester wags his head. "You see one, you kill it, pretty simple."

***

Living and working in the Yaak makes a person consider many things before venturing out into wild lands. Getting eaten is one worry. Hungry grizzly bears weigh hundreds of pounds. Mountain lions see humans as portable meat packets.

Getting stomped by a breeding bull moose causes more worry.

Being stabbed by sharp pointy antlers is another.

But, above all else, one creature strikes deadly fear in the hearts of hard timber beasts and loggers.

It weighs in at a fearsome ten to twenty pounds with short little legs, a round little body, and a pointed little nose.

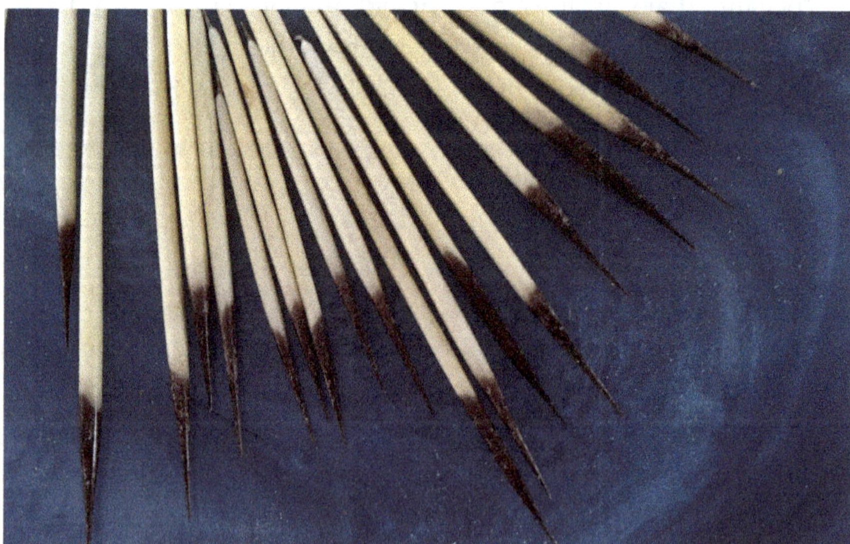

Porcupine quills were used extensively in Native America Dress.

It's innocent in its being, but its protective shell of over thirty thousand sharp pointed quills is deadly. Each quill has seven to eight hundred microscopic barbs along the tip.

Scientists call it Erethizon dorsatum. Native Americans say Pahin, ts'I. Loggers and foresters call them quill pigs.

The dreaded porcupine.

Terror of the woods.

Bane of the forest industry.

The stuff of nightmares for foresters and loggers.

These little vegetarians eat the sweet cambium layer of young trees. That tasty goodness between the outer bark and the wood is a mainstay of their diets. They strip many trees in their lifetime.

But even tastier is road sign wood glue. No sign is safe from the porcupine's appetite.

In the late seventies and early eighties, quill pigs were everywhere. Because they're slow moving on the roads, they're vulnerable to humans. People would throw a coat over the critter, or just kill them to get their quills.

It's all about the quills.

Despite folk legends, quills do not shoot out like arrows. But they do come loose when touched. Then those hundreds of tiny barbs dig in.

I became an expert in removing quills because of my not-very-smart doggie that refused to leave the little critters alone. Since I lived a long way from a vet, I became very efficient at removing quills. More than once, neighbors called me to remove quills from their various dogs, also.

When a dog tries to bite a porcupine, quills become imbedded in the roof of the dog's mouth. Then they break off and thousands of barbs work their way in deeper. That's the worst, not fun at all for the poor dog.

The little creatures can cause excruciating pain, but they are also important to Native American life. Humility and modesty are qualities that Salish peoples saw in the porcupine.

Porcupine quill art is unique to Native Americans. Quills are dyed with native berries and used as tools. It's hard to imagine a Native American ceremonial outfit that does not include these colorful quills.

But, these days, porcupines are rare.

"Seen a porcupine in a while?" I often ask Yaak locals.

"Nope, not in a while," is the usual reply.

The little vegetarians have all but vanished from the mountainous timber land of western Montana. They are still doing well on the plains of Eastern Montana. But, in the west, few are spotted.

No one knows for sure why.

Maybe disease.

Or an increase in predators, like the elusive fisher that's known to cleverly roll the little guys over to get to their soft underbellies.

Maybe loss of habitat due to climate change.

Or humans with twenty-two pistols or shovels to whack them.

Maybe it was just time to move on to the east side with fewer tourists.

There's a yin and yang in everything.

One the good side, the disappearance of porcupines means I no longer have to deal with quills in the noses of silly doggies.

But, on the other side, it's sad that their small but important position in this fragile world is gone.

In our wild timber lands, the porcupine's humility and modesty are lost.

***

The newbie forester grips the shovel handle tighter and steadies herself to obey her boss's dreaded orders.

But...wait.

It's gone, scurried off in the underbrush.

The cute little mad max creature must have sensed death

coming and found safety. It will survive another day.

The new forester leans on her shovel and smiles.

PART ONE

Three Paws

Log truck drivers call him Old Three Paws because of his limp. No one knows how he was injured. Forest Service say every spring for years he had been breaking into the old Pete Cabin where they found blood on the window spikes. He was one big ass grumpy grizzly. Drivers bet on who would get his hide on their wall. A tag for a grizzly bear was a fifty-dollar bill.

Three Paws was not a happy bear. Old age does that to you. His front paw was bothering him, and his winter had been unsettled. For many years, his winter home was a den in the high basin of the lakes. But now, from time to time, the earth shook beneath his den. That made him restless.

On a sunny spring morning, he emerged from his den and expelled his fecal plug. Then he started looking for food. Any food.

The smell of man was everywhere. At a man camp, a discarded old sardine can wasn't much food. Other garbage smells caught his nose but nothing to feed on.

Maybe a good rub on his favorite tree would improve his mood. But he couldn't find it. It had been taken.

75

The trees were gone. The land he'd roamed for years looked different.

The world of old Three Paws was changing. And not for the better.

***

Three a.m. alarm.

On the road before four a.m., Justin shifts gears in his 1959 Peterbilt logging truck, now three years old. On the seat beside him sits a beat-up Stanley thermos of coffee and fried eggs on Wonder bread.

Forty-thirty a.m., he turns up the one-lane gnarly ass Yaak 508 road. He calls out over the CB, "Two mile up the Yaak empty."

Still early but better start calling out mile markers. Even at this hour, you never know who's coming down.

It's been a tough week hauling logs for Justin. The miles are long, and a couple of breakdowns left him behind on the load count. He hopes to pick up that up today.

He's brought his secret weapon.

"Dead man's curve coming up empty," Justin calls over the CB. This spot has earned its name. In daylight, it's bad enough but, in the dark, with the waters of the Yaak running high right on the edge, it's spooky.

Once he's passed, he breathes a sigh of relief and unclenches his white knuckles from the wheel.

Five a.m., he turns up the new Pete Creek Road. Twenty-two miles of dirt road to the unit. His truck is already starting to show the wear. Saturday will be a welding day. Logging is tough on everything. Them trees don't go easily. And there are a lot of spruce trees still left to go.

***

In 1948, a massive wind event knocked down thousands of acres of timber in the Yaak.

What happens to a bunch of dead trees lying around? They get bugs. Lots of them. Dendroctonus rufipennis to Foresters. Spruce beetle to everyone else. Native bugs were spreading like never before.

What happens when a Forest Service forester sees lots of bugs in the woods? Every crazy logging idea imaginable.

The Yaak Foresters hatched a plan. Cut every infested spruce tree. And for the heck of it, just cut every spruce tree you can. So what if spruce grows mostly at high elevations? If there is a single spruce tree in that high mountain basin, by God, we will build a road to it. And they did.

In 1954, a massive road building program hit the Yaak. They brought in bulldozers on steroids.

If you've ever hiked on a Yaak hiking trail, it probably started out as a bulldozer road to log spruce trees.

***

Justin downshifts to start the climb and calls over the CB, "Ten mile headed up the Pete Crick grade."

As he crests the grade and gets to the Pete Creek Meadows, he sees Old Three Paws, limping through long grass, confirming the rumors he's been hearing from other drivers. In the early light, he makes out the graying hump and dark hide of the massive old grizzly, moving into the lodgepole pine.

After Justin crosses the West Fork of the Yaak, he drives by the first cutting unit. The logging units are massive, miles long. No environmental rules here. Fear of bugs makes the Foresters do crazy stuff.

Bulldozers skid giant spruce through creeks, steams, swamps, over hills and over dales and everywhere in between. Spruce is in demand for a growing California. They even built the world's biggest airplane, the Spruce Goose, with spruce plywood.

Justin finally makes it to the landing near Hawkins Lake. The timber fallers are falling the largest spruce near the lake. Big money is in big wood.

Rubin, the loader operator, and Justin exchange morning gossip.

"I saw Three Paws in the Meadows this morning," Justin says. "That's one big bear."

"Hope no one messes with him," Rubin says. "Not too many old ones left." Rubin grew up on a local homestead and loves all the wild creatures.

"Say," Justin says, "I'm starting to fall behind in the load count because of the distance. Wonder if maybe I could get a few whiskey loads today to help me catch up." He hands over his secret weapon--a fifth of Rubin's favorite weekend whiskey.

Rubin smiles. "Whiskey loads, it is."

Whiskey loads are the biggest logs. Quicker to load, quicker to unload. Equals more loads.

Beer loads are smaller trees. Takes forever to load and unload. Equals a pain in the ass day.

***

Grizzly photo by BJ Johnson.

Three Paws was one of the last survivors in a world that was no longer his. As he roamed his changed landscape, man was everywhere he went. But the grizzly was alone.

One might hope he went peacefully into the night. Sadly, he did not. When the Forest Service arrived next spring to open the Pete Creek work cabin, they found it had been broken into once again by Three Paws.

Not far from the cabin was his body, curled up in a ball. The Forest Service had left rat poison out and the big bruin ate it all. He died a horrible and agonizing death just like the spruce forest he used to roam.

Some folks shed a tear for a great, beautiful, wild Yaak life that is gone for the old spruce forest and an old grizzly bear with a limp.

Spruce logging in the Yaak lasted well into the late '70s. Those who toiled in the woods bought homes and, for the first time, sent their daughters and sons to college. Friends and I took advantage of the miles of plowed winter roads to ski the high basins.

In 2017, a spruce tree from the Yaak became the National Christmas Tree. Spruce trees again grow big around here.

There is a new thought in the world of tree whisperers and scientists that all trees are connected somehow through their roots. Alive and dead. Hopefully the young spruce trees that have regenerated will connect with the stumps of their ancestors to continue to tell their story of survival.

One can only hope that the offspring of Three Paws are out there somewhere carrying on his story of survival.

PART ONE

Guardian Angels

In the early 1980s, my job was a Fuel Technician working in the fire shop for the Forest Service out of the Sylvanite Ranger Station. Sounds complicated but, basically, I wandered over hill and dale of the Yaak, counting sticks. Big sticks, little sticks, sticks that were alive and sticks that were dead. I weighed sticks for moisture content. I measured sticks for size. I figured out what kind of sticks they were.

The Yaak has a lot of sticks. When I found the right combination of sticks, we'd go burn the crap out of it.

I also did initial attacks for wildfires in the north end of the district. When smoke was spotted, basically, I'd get there as fast as I could and figure out what was up.

That day, the voice of Shamus called over the radio from the Mount Henry Lookout. "I got it in the northeast quarter of the northwest quarter of section six. Township thirty-seven north, Range thirty-two west, over."

"Roger that," I called back. "Sounds like it's up north as I check my map. I'll start heading that way, over." I welcomed the change in routine from stick counting.

Lookout Shamus called back, "Starting to get a lot more smoke. I think it's right on the border, over."

"I'm up the North Fork of Beetle Creek," I answered. "I must drop down to Pete Creek and head for the West Fork, right? Over."

"West Fork would be my guess." Lookout Shamus radios. "Been watching a thunderstorm build up that way for awhile, guess it let loose, over."

There was a certain comfort in a lookout's voice that's hard to describe. When I found myself out in the middle of frigging nowhere, it was reassuring to know Mount Henry Shamus was watching over me.

He was the perfect lookout person. With experience in wildland fire fighting and the calmness of a musician, his voice was perfect over the radio. He worked both the Baldy Mountain lookout and the Mount Henry lookout.

When I wandered in the woods counting sticks, on many days he was my only contact with the outside world. Check in first thing in the morning, lunch, and when done. He would always be there. Lookout extraordinaire, sawyer, firefighter, stand-up bass player, poet, and a long-time resident of the Yaak. Friend and neighbor in this remote world.

Mount Henry was Shamus's second home, a home he cared for. During my supply and check-in runs to the lookout, everything was always in order. Lookout painted, windows clean, and nothing out of place. That impressed me.

Shamus loved his second home. And he loved when visitors came by, and he could explain the world of a lookout.

I radioed back, "I'm going to be dropping into Pete Creek and then up the West Fork so won't be able to hear dispatch. Will need to relay through you I think, over."

"I'm here for you, buddy. Be safe, over," Shamus answered.

With those simple words, I knew he would be there as always.

Mount Henry Lookout in winter.

He would have my back until I got home.

Another part of my job was what's called a smoke chaser. I carried a smoke chaser pack in my pickup with everything needed to fight a small fire. When smoke was detected on the north end of the district, off I went.

Wandering the wild lands of the Yaak looking for a single burning tree was not an easy task. Brush overhead and timber reaching the sky, I sometimes wondered where the heck I was.

The Yaak has been called the asbestos district. When lightning struck a single tree, wet brush and soggy ground often kept fires limited to that small area. I'd get so soaked, splashing my way to find the sputtering fire, that I'd have to rekindle flames to warm up before I put the fire out. Funny place, this Yaak.

Not this day, though. As I topped off the Pete Creek Road, I saw three different lighting strikes throwing up smoke as more strikes came down.

I drove as far as the U.S.-Canadian border and called over the radio, "This thunderstorm is throwing out some strikes and the winds are strong. Got some locations for you, over."

"Go ahead, will relay, over," Mount Henry responded.

"Some fire on the ground is starting to spread." I radioed details to my lookout guardian to relay. "Got one fire burning on both sides of the border with some crowning in the trees. Can I still cross the border? Over." I didn't want to be arrested. Back in the day, many logging roads went right to the border and we'd fight fires without worrying about an imaginary line.

"Dispatch says the cross-border agreement is still in place," Mount Henry replied. "No worries, over."

I added, "Better get the helicopter moving, got some smokes way up the hillsides. Also tell them the winds are intense. Might have to set down at Upper Ford until it calms down, over."

"Will do, the winds are strong up here too. Gusty to thirty-five plus on the gauge. Will keep you posted, over."

Mount Henry had become the local dispatcher, weather station and guardian of firefighters.

I located and called in four additional fires, two of which soon became one.

In the beginning, that first half hour was always fun and exciting. Arriving at the unknown. Is it a small tree or a towering inferno? Decisions to make. Should I deal with it myself or call for help? What resources are needed? Remembering training and doing what I could do effectively.

Really the best time.

The rest of firefighting is just backbreaking hard work. Plain and simple.

While I figured out what the best course was, I received another call from Mount Henry.

"I got a Canadian retardant bomber who is listening in," Mount Henry lookout radioed. "He wants to know if you need a drop. He's working another fire nearby, over."

Shamus on Mount Henry is now an international flight director. How cool was that.

At that moment, I was alone and out gunned. "It would sure help right now, over."

"Okay, he's on his way. Said he would make a pass with his siren on and do the drop on the second pass." Shamus added, "Remember the last time, these guys come in low so keep your head down. Be safe, over."

Soon other resources started showing up with radios that could reach the Forest dispatch, so the Mount Henry relay was no longer needed. But Shamus would remain there in the background, watching over us.

More than once over the years, I found myself a long way from nowhere, working a fire in the middle of the night. Shamus was there with that calm voice, an ever-present lookout guardian, giving me comfort in the darkness of the wilderness.

Back then, if you lived in the wild woodlands, you understood the importance of a guardian on a tower with a warm voice. Sad to say, the Mount Henry lookout has now been abandoned and is falling into major disrepair.

But I still remember the comfort that Shamus used to give to a wandering fuel tech, along with reassurance and security to ranchers and loggers of the Yaak. More than once, locals asked me if that old man Shamus was in his Mount Henry perch, keeping watch.

"He sure is," I answered. "Keeping an eye on this place."

"Good, we sleep better at night knowing he's up there."

Higher praise could not be given.

PART ONE

Faith and Trust

Living in the remote Yaak, a dog comes in handy as a friend and guardian.

Their jobs range from a bear alarm to a fitness reminder. "You're getting lazy and I need a walk."

Montanans have house dogs, cow dogs, family dogs, bear dogs, truck dogs, RV dogs, and more.

Then there's the trail dog. That dog is special. For me, it is about faith. Not faith in your dog but in yourself. Faith that you have done all you can do to make him trust you. Trust that your dog comes every time you call because he wants to.

A trail dog knows the difference between a mailbox walk and a hike. He knows when you put on those dusty hiking boots, when you pull the pack down and start loading goodies. He knows he's about to have a very good day.

Our trail dog is Famous Amos. We got him as a rescue from the reservation when he was four months old. Sleek and red with the face of a fox and no idea what breed he is. No love in his puppy life, running wild and scared.

Doubtful folks said, "He'll never be trainable, too aggressive. Don't waste your time trying."

But you know what? Time is the great healer. That, plus biscuits!

We worked hard to bring stability and trust to his life.

Love, training, and biscuits. Love, training, and biscuits. Over and over with patience and consistency.

At a certain point, something happened.

All that love, training, and biscuits worked. We replaced his fear with faith. Faith that we would be there for him. And, with his newfound trust, he decided he liked us. The fun began.

Amos knows when it's time. He sits by the truck making sure we don't leave him at home. We take him everywhere.

When we hiked into the Wave in Utah, people told him that he was famous for being there. It went to his head. From then on, I had to call him Famous Amos.

At home, he can sometimes be a real butt head. Squirrels will always be an issue. He just can't help it. But on the trail, he's different.

Hiking in the Yaak is not like most places. In 40+ years hiking here, I've seen about six people on trails and not a soul in the last six years. Lots of critters, few people. Trailheads are hard to find and sometimes it's nearly impossible to tell the real trail from a deer trail. But Amos knows.

At the trailhead, we let Amos out to roam around first to make sure it's safe. When he's satisfied, he stands at the trailhead, looking back at us. Time to go, he says. We put a small bell on him. That warns critters and lets us know where he is so we don't have to yell for him.

Once we're on the trail, he's different. He becomes the guardian, more tentative, responsive, always keeping us in sight even when he's 50 feet ahead, out on point, scouting for us. If we stop to check out a plant, he returns to check on us.

He always knows who carries his lunch and water.

Amos, Edd's faithful companion.

At the end of the trail, when we're standing around enjoying refreshments, he leans against me. I think maybe he smiles about the very good day we had, with faith and trust that we'll have many more.

PART ONE

Wild Eyes

The stink eye stare down has been going on for too long. One of us has to make a move soon for the sake of survival. His more than mine. But nobody is moving.

The greedy interloper has disrupted a beautiful morning of fishing on the Yaak River with filtered light and the lapping rhythm of summer's water.

Before I can make a move, he goes first.

A quick launch with a sharp veer to the left catches me off guard. A steep dive takes him down out of reach. Before I react, he rises out of the water with a two-inch-long fish and lands on the nearest branch.

A quick flip of the head and down the gullet goes the fish.

With a wink and a stare, the Belted Kingfisher tells me, That's how it's done, amateur.

Really not fair, I tell him. You catch them underwater.

Why is staring into wild eyes so intriguing?

Domestic animal eyes are different. The liquid brown eyes of a dog say it all, I love you and bacon and sausage and walks and petting and just about everything you do.

Wild animal eyes aren't the same. When they stare at you, you can't help but wonder what they're thinking. You're either a curiosity or food. Probably both. Mostly food, I think.

Living in the wilderness of the Yaak I am blessed to have more wild animal neighbors than human neighbors.

Human eyes are confusing because they change depending on where you meet them. In cities, eye contact is avoided because of the fear of what it might bring. In the country, it's different because there aren't too many human eyes around. The ones you see are the ones you know.

Wild animal eyes have other meanings that vary from curiosity to fear to you look like a corn dog. That is, if they know what a corn dog looks like.

Big brown deer eyes are the most innocent, staring in amazement at everything.

Moose eyes say, I'm the biggest thing around so don't bother me. If you're eye to eye with a moose, believe him or else.

Elk have the wary eyes of survivors that keep them alive.

Bear eyes are curious, usually accompanied by a twitching nose. Is that huckleberry pie I smell?

The saddest wild eyes I ever saw belonged to an ancient, crippled black bear that had made its way into one of our apple trees. When I went to shoo him away, all I saw were the weathered, gray, and tired eyes of a creature on his last days, probably eating the last apples of his life.

Cat eyes. I once stared into the eyes of an elusive lynx. They were intense, then gone in a flash.

Coyote eyes are intriguing. Behind those eyes is a brain that likes to play games right out of the comics.

The only eyes that have caused serious concern belonged to a rare and elusive creature. Working in the woods sometimes required a bit of bushwhacking through wilderness. The only way across a good size creek was over an old log jam. As I stepped onto it, up popped a full-grown wolverine on the opposite side.

Okay, now what?

I'm not sure what was worse, the rank smell or staring into those dark beady eyes. This animal was the undisputed king of its wilderness world.

Wolverines are true meat eaters. And I was a tall meat packet. Breakfast, lunch, and dinner.

Luckily, he decided to go the other way. When I later hiked out, there was no repeat encounter. Whew.

The next morning when I hiked in, boom, there he was again, stinking and hanging out in the middle of the log jam. Uh-oh.

All I could think of was the story of Robin Hood and Friar Tuck fighting to cross a log.

The very stinky stare down dragged on, with me worried it wouldn't end well. Yet, I couldn't move because this was a rare, special moment. A wolverine and me.

Luckily, he realized I meant no harm, moved away, and allowed me to cross.

I'll never forget the eyes of that truly wild creature.

Red eyes in darkness. You really don't want to see them at night in your headlamp. They're never comforting. Instead, they add a giddy up to your step. Whether they belong to skunks or wolves, red eyes evoke memories of werewolves and childhood fears of the dark.

Next chance you have, study those eyes from the wilderness. Whether big, brown, and innocent or dark, beady, and menacing, they're intriguing. Imagine what they're telling you. Mostly likely, they're hoping to see food.

PART ONE

The Grub Stake

"CRACK!"

A trigger pulled!

A bullet launched!

A 165 grain, 30.06 bullet travels at 2850 feet per second.

With luck, impact will be in 0.08 of a second.

The day starts at four a.m., way too early, but par for the course this time of year. Lunch packed and an egg sandwich for the drive, then I'm on the road up Fourth of July Creek arriving by five a.m. at the Tepee Mountain saddle.

It's the weekend after Thanksgiving Day and the last day of hunting season.

But no meat in the freezer yet.

A little worried but a lot of daylight to go so I'm not panicked just yet.

People who don't hunt have a hard time understanding the importance of wild meat in the freezer. Not only helps the budget but, more important, the protein keeps you alive during those long

Yaak winters. That's a comfort. Plus, it makes some pretty good tacos on Taco Tuesday.

Most of the world buys their food on a daily pace.

Remote rural lifestyles do not. This place I call home is that way. Jaunts to town can be an hour, or two, or more and are really grubstake trips to stock up. Not one dozen eggs, but five dozen at a time. Four gallons of milk, not one. Everything bought in super-sized quantities. Extra refrigerators and freezers are common. Some friends literally buy six months of food at a time.

The day already seems long and it's still dark at five-thirty when I park my rig at the pull out. My hike starts, wearing a headlamp, trudging up the hill through calf-deep snow and blow down lodge pole. A half hour trek in the dark to the ridge top overlooking the river.

Not a bad place to watch the morning break.

0.04 of a second to impact.

As I settle into a view spot in fresh snow with my back up against a beautiful western larch tree, I find myself in my own little heaven. Nothing like watching a sunrise from a ridge line above the river, light snow falling. It is turning into a perfect day.

I spend the day slowly working the ridge line. I spot three mule deer does. Not legal this time of year.

Four cow elk walk within thirty yards while I'm eating lunch. Never ever saw me. Also, not legal.

The term grubstake was first used in early mining days when a miner would find someone to finance his claim in return for a share of the gold. Eventually the term came to mean the supplies one needed to make it through the winter.

In homestead days, settlers set forest fires in hopes the Forest Service would hire them and provide their winter grubstake money. It occurred often enough that, in some areas, mountains have been called Grubstake Mountain.

I work my way back down the ridge and settle into a tree well to wait until dark before hiking to my rig. For the last half hour, I've been lying still in the snow and am frozen stiff. The day is fading and still no grubstake.

Maybe it's time to start panicking. Just a little.

As I'm ready to call it quits, a band of mule deer come into view on the ridge and hunker in below me. I can see antlers on one but can't see his body. I settle my scope on the antlers and the wait begins.

The grubstake requires many pieces to survive. In the fall, the garden rewards need to be preserved and stored. Wild berries and herbs are gathered, packaged, and stored. A trip to town for baking supplies and extras.

Now that work is done.

All that's needed is a harvest of deer or elk to complete our winter grubstake.

As dusk settles, I can only make out the antlers through my scope. Still no movement. I am cold, tired, hungry, and stiff from lying still so long that I may not be able to rise. Only minutes left between legal light and darkness.

Never owned a gun until I came to the Yaak and now I'm eager for winter protein.

Hunting is more than just protein. It's heritage. It's about family and friends reconnecting each year, bonding at hunting camp. It's about grandpa showing his grandkids his favorite whitetail spot under that larch tree to take a nap. Hunting is a basic part of life here.

There's a saying that if you haven't filled your deer tag by the last week, head to the Yaak. Locals say, "You're bound to shoot something."

It has always been about the meat. My wife says, "Can't eat horns."

My last opportunity for this fall. It's time.

A trigger pulled.

A bullet launched.

0.08 of a second later.

Whack.

Impact.

A mule deer buck down.

As darkness settles in, I find him with the light in my headlamp, right where he rested. I give thanks to him, and the world I live in.

I get to work, glad I put fresh batteries in my headlamp.

As I flounder down the ridge toward my rig, guided by headlamp through blow down timber and fresh snow with an overloaded pack of meat, I realize I am in heaven. My type of heaven. Of course, my wife will worry because it's late, but she'll be pleased with winter meat. Love that Taco Tuesday.

The grubstake is complete.

PART ONE

A Simple Line

"One step."

"Two step."

"Three step."

"Four," I mumble to myself as the rhyme of movement carries me forward.

"One step."

"Two step."

"Three step."

"Four step more." I repeat to myself as the fresh powder gets deeper and not a whole lot lighter.

There's a rhythm to breaking fresh trails through Rocky Mountain powder. A rhythm of wandering thoughts and fleeting ideas but, always, the rhythm of forward movement must continue. The line must continue forward and upward.

Some of my ski partners claim I break a narrow track. They could be right, an old habit from learning to backcountry ski in Sierra Mountain cement in the seventies. I like my track. Straight and clean with less resistance.

"One step."

"Two step."

"Three step."

"Four step, there's donkeys at the door," I mumble to myself.

Donkeys at the door? Maybe it's time to pass the lead to someone else.

Not quite yet.

If you don't back country ski, you won't understand the feel or joy of breaking a trail through an expanse of virgin powder. You are the first to be there. The first to lay down tracks into the unknown. Only you know how this path will go. Should I steepen the track or keep going at a gentle rise?

I should give up the lead, fall in behind, and bring up the rear. Pretty nice track in the back.

Not quite yet.

The line must go forward and upwards.

Making ski tracks up Roderick Mountain.

"One step."

"Two step."

"Three step."

"Four step, there's two donkeys at the door," I think to myself.

Need a new rhyme.

The snow is perfect. Fresh and clean and all mine. My ski waxing has been perfect. With exact downward pressure with the ball of my foot, I launch forward ever so slightly. Always forward. Always upward.

It's lonely at the front, they say. Not here, not now. As I move, I focus on my ski tips buried under that pure white blanket and hope they stay straight and true. Really haven't seen them for some time. While I hear faint voices behind, I am alone in my own home of pure whiteness.

There is nothing purer than a foot of fresh Rocky Mountain powder. And you are the first to lay down your mark. In the world of downhill skiing, they talk about their favorite lines down the mountain. In the quiet world of backcountry travel, there are two lines. The one down, but the line up is the one that really counts.

"One step."

"Two step."

"Three step."

"Four step."

The line must be perfect. Not too steep for those that follow but always upward. Always upwards towards that reward you seek at the end of the line. Many different joys await at line's end.

Cocktails on the deck of the Mount Henry lookout. Lunch on the Montana- Idaho border with views of Northwest Peaks. Or just spending the day on the open eastern slopes of Roderick Mountain.

"One step."

"Two step."

"Hey, quit daydreaming." I hear friends following behind. "Let someone else break trail for a while. You can't have all the fun."

I step aside and fall in at the back. My line is over for now but the line itself continues forward and upwards. Always forward and upwards.

PART ONE

A Christmas Healing

The journey had been hard. She was young and strong when they started. Now she was just young. When they began, there were five in the clan. Three males, the herd mother, and her. Two of the clan were lost to wolves in north Idaho. She last saw her mate defending her from a mountain lion while crossing the Moyie River where she was cut.

Last night, as they climbed to the ridge that divides Idaho and Montana, the herd matron gave her a look that said she could go no further and wandered off to find her peace.

Now she was alone but could not stop moving. She could not explain it. She just had to keep moving forward. Her body felt changes because of what she carried. Didn't know why. Just keep moving.

At the ridge that protects the Yaak, she smelled it. The special place. She could smell the old ones. The silent ancient ones. As she moved down hill into the Yaak, the snow became deeper, but her wide hooves made walking easier.

The old growth of the Yaak. The land of giants, where cedar, hemlock, spruce, and white pine dominated. The place that fed the herd with arboreal lichen. The guardians that sheltered her mother when she was born.

She couldn't explain it, but this was the place where she must deliver, her reason for coming. She was pregnant and for all she knew the last of her kind. Alone in the world.

As the snow came down, frost was building on her nose. She knew she had to stop. This was where her life began.

But it was different now.

There was a man thing there now.

Too tired to go any farther, she sought safety from the storm in the walls of a shelter. She was done.

***

The girls had been fighting for days, it seemed. They were angry, confused. They couldn't understand why their daddy had to die.

Things had been rough since last spring after the logging accident up Pete Creek. Kathryn knew in time things would heal, but the tears still came too easy. One moment, life grew and thrived, the next, sadness and tears in a life with no purpose.

Money was scarce. All the animals had been sold to put together their winter grubstake but that reserve grew smaller each day. She got some work caring for the dying wife of her elderly neighbor Amos. But not much since the woman's passing. The chickens still gave eggs, but they were slowly becoming dinner.

Kathryn worried. She always worried these days. Christmas was coming and she wanted to do something for her girls to make their lives better.

One snowy December morning, the girls went out to gather eggs. Moments later, they rushed into the kitchen with no eggs, talking over each other.

"Mom, Mom, there's a reindeer in the shed."

She gave them a scolding look. "It's not nice to make up stories."

"Really, really, Mommy. It's hurt. Please come."

Kathryn put on her winter coat and boots to see this reindeer.

When she got there, all she could do was stare. A buck of some sort? Not like any deer she had ever seen. Not even the wild stories she'd heard from the old timers.

Caribou, that's what they were called. A caribou lay in her shed, hurt and very fat.

Most homesteaders would have seen this as easy winter meat. Kathryn was not one of them. She loved the wildlife in her world and hated killing for sport.

For a few seconds, she watched the rhythm of its breathing. Wounds had come from some attack. Having raised many farm animals, Kathryn knew the caribou was pregnant.

It was way too early for spring babies, but this mom was in trouble. Her baby would arrive soon.

Realization struck Kathryn. This amazing creature had come to them for a reason, to give them a purpose. This was a blessing. Not a burden.

She knelt and gathered her girls in her arms. "We've been given a very special Christmas gift. We're going to help this beautiful creature."

As she looked back and forth between her daughters' faces, she recognized the sparkle in their eyes that she had not seen in a long time. Smiles of joy lifted the dark shadow that had been over them.

Kathryn knew how to deal with farm animals but not a wild caribou. She needed advice. Amos! Their neighbor and family friend whom she trusted.

Amos had come to the Yaak at 16 and had lived there for more than 60 years. She'd gotten to know the stubborn, opinionated, self-sufficient homesteader as they worked together, caring for his wife. He would give Kathryn the faded plaid shirt off his back if she needed it. Amos would know what to do.

She hurried to his log home, bigger and sturdier than hers, and told him the story.

"You have a what in the barn?"

"I know my animals, and this is a caribou!" She grasped his sinewy arm and tugged him back to her barn.

At first, all he could do was stare. "It's a god dang pregnant caribou."

It lay on its side, not moving but breathing, the girls flanking it at a respectful distance.

Amos looked over his spectacles at Kathryn. "You know," he said, "most people would see this as winter meat."

Kathryn's jaw set firm, her eyes narrowed with a furrow in her brow. "We are not those people."

Her steady, determined stare must have convinced him he had to help. He squatted a few feet from the caribou. "This is what to do with wild animals. Go slowly. Be calm. Earn her trust. Kathryn, do you have those native plants you dried a while back?"

She nodded and retrieved a glass jar from the kitchen. He showed her and the girls how to make a healing salve.

Next, he faced the girls. "From what I've heard, caribou only eat the moss that we call old man's beard. It grows on the spruce and hemlock. You girls go collect some."

For the next few hours, they went slow, their touch gentle.

***

The journey had taken all her strength. Her time was soon. When the people first came into the shelter, a moment of panic urged her to run. But she had no strength left. All she could do was breathe.

She felt calmness in the woman and hidden strength. Her touch was gentle, soft. The girls and a quiet old man hung old blankets across the openings to keep the cold out.

Gradually, a bond formed between the healer and the injured. They all waited for the day.

***

Christmas morning dawned crisp and cold with a foot of new

snow. Kathryn and her daughters tiptoed to the shed. The caribou struggled to her feet, breathing hard. Standing on shaky legs, she delivered her baby.

Kathryn clasped a hand of each daughter and murmured, "This could be one of the last caribou. This is our holiday gift."

The new mother licked and nudged her child to its feet. Its mouth fumbled along her underbelly and began to nurse.

One daughter whispered, "Mom, can we name it?"

"No, this a child of the wild and not ours to name. The mother's strength will come back, and her baby will grow." Kathryn squeezed her girls' hands. "Soon they'll move on. They must."

***

The new year started clear and not so cold. The girls came running into the kitchen from outside, chattering and laughing. "Mom, there's another one on the hill behind the cabin."

Kathryn followed them outside. "Sure enough, that's another caribou," she said. "Isn't he proud and strong? Maybe he's from the same herd."

They walked to the shed and Kathryn reached up to unfasten the blankets. "It's time, girls." She folded the blankets as the new mother and baby wandered outside. The mother spotted the caribou on the hill and raised her beautiful head as if she recognized him.

"Maybe that's her mate," Kathryn said. "She and her winter baby won't be alone."

They watched the pair move into the shadows of the ancient ones. The mother turned back for a brief second and her eyes met Kathryn's. In those eyes, Kathryn felt warmth into her heart. Tears spilled but they were tears of joy.

The care and love they used to heal a wild creature also healed their own wounded hearts. They were still poor but stronger as a family like never before.

A few days later, Amos stopped by to check in.

When they told him the caribou had left, he said, "They must keep moving. It's in their makeup. Their journey must go on."

He shifted one foot to the other.

"What is it, Amos?" Kathryn asked.

"Kathryn, this is not a marriage proposal. But I want to make you an offer."

The girls gasped. Kathryn shushed them. "Go on, Amos."

"My doctors tell me my time is coming to an end. After my wife died, I just gave up caring. I have no family so the ranch will just be sold to some developer and divided up. To be honest I'm lonely in that big house. Here's my offer. You and the girls move in with me and help. In return, before I pass, I'll sign over the ranch to you and the girls."

Now it was Kathryn's turn to gasp. "Why me?"

"Remember when I said most people would kill that injured caribou? I saw that look in your eye. There's strength in you, Kathryn, plus a whole lot of love for this place we call the Yaak. I need help and you need help." He hesitated with a sigh. "I just don't want to die alone."

So, with a handshake, the deal was done.

Amos lived his last days in a house filled with laughter. He passed surrounded by love and compassion.

In the years that followed, Kathryn and her daughters became successful ranchers and prominent residents in the Yaak. Every winter, they remembered the gift from the Christmas caribou.

PART ONE

The Soul of a Place

Pastor Eli speaks: "It's alive, I tell ya."

"What's alive?" asks Bert, his drinking partner.

"This place we live in. This Yaak place we call home."

"It's alive, you say. What's alive?" Bert asks, confused and a little buzzed from Eli's home brew.

"I've been pondering this thought for longer than I can remember," says the Pastor, as he calls himself these days. "I'm pretty sure this place we live in is a living, breathing self-sustaining life form."

Bert has to admit, he really enjoys his once-a-month get-together with his neighbor and friend of more than forty years. After a few home brews, you never know where the talk is headed.

Bert met Eli when Eli first moved into the North Fork of the Yaak, as far away from the real world as you can imagine. Bought ten acres along the creek and built a plastic lean-to to survive in that first winter. And survive he did. Built a cabin from trees off the land and put in a garden for vegetables. He lived his life the way he wanted, simple and with limited burdens.

Work came in many forms, tree planter, tree thinner, and a walker of the woods. His favorite type of work was what's called "Stand Exams." Working under Forest Service contracts, he would wander the woods, measuring trees and doing habitat typing of the woods. Basically, looking at what the heck is out there.

But Eli's true passion lies in botanical gathering. The collection and selling of products of the natural world. Few people know how many everyday things come from the world of nature. From huckleberries sold to bakeries, from plant seeds supplied to nurseries, from small aspens delivered to landscapers, from yew brush and other plants used for cancer medicine, And, of course, morel mushrooms that restaurants paid a fair price for. He even found out about the native plant that is the secret ingredient in a popular soft drink.

The natural world gives him his livelihood. He knows how to harvest responsibly and respect the plants. No rakes when he harvests berries. He hand-picks to avoid damaging the plants. He takes only a few seeds so others will continue to grow.

He knows the bad reputations some botanical gatherers have. Like entire hillsides in Oregon and Washington stripped of bear grass for flower arrangements. Or over-harvesting rare live plants for the latest "Native Plant" craze for home gardens. He is not that type of gatherer. He loves and cares for this place he bonded with long ago.

"Another brew?" The pastor asks.

"Sounds good." Bert knows he has only a short walk down the cutoff road.

Bert can't really remember when Eli became Pastor Eli. Probably at one of their home-brewed get-togethers. Or maybe from his lonely wanderings in the wilderness. Eli disappears for days, living off what this one-of-a-kind place gives him.

With the latest wave of new folks moving in and the tourists' numbers growing every summer, he has found a whole new career:

a guide for Forest Bathing tours. He also found out that for only $29.99, he could start his own church.

The Church of the Quiet Wild.

Every church needs a spiritual leader, so Eli became Pastor Eli.

Because of his unique experience living and learning to understand the heartbeat and breath of this place, and because he lives in the heart of God's country, he has become a person in demand. People pay him real money to take them into the woods and sit on a log and bathe in the woods around them. Because his tours occur on National Forest Service land, he operates under a special use permit. He recently applied for a permit to do winter bathing tours. Sit on a frozen log to take in winter's solitude.

A new world for sure.

Pastor Eli starts to elaborate: "I've wandered from the Selkirk Mountains in the north, to where the Yaak River dumps into the Kootenai River. From the Mount Henry and the Purcell Divide in the East to Northwest Peaks and Newton Ridge in the west. It's isolated from the rest of the world around it."

"You do like to wander a bit, that's for sure," Bert agrees.

"Think about it," Eli says. "The Yaak is just like a human body. It's wrapped in the mountains around it so it's like a separate body from the rest of the outside world around it. It has everything a human body has. Its rocky crags and rolling hills are its sturdy bones. Its heavy timber stands are like its protective skin. But, most importantly, like any living thing, it needs its own separate blood system. And this place has been blessed with an abundance. The Yaak's many streams and creeks are its flowing veins. Remember, they originate in the Yaak Valley ecosystem. Like a separate body."

Bert notices the passion for this place surging in Pastor Eli's voice.

"With this abundance of blood, there must be a heart. A quiet moment by creek, a sunrise from a ridge line, or just sitting at the base of a Mother Tree pondering its life. You can feel its heartbeat, and, if you're lucky, its soul at times like this. The bathing times." The Pastor speaks in all seriousness.

Bert listens as he gulps more brew.

"What happens when you get a heartbeat and flowing blood?" The Pastor goes on. "You get life. An abundance of life. It takes a lot of little pieces for something to be alive. Same with our little world. From the smallest mushrooms and wildflowers to its largest and tallest timber. The very little creatures to our grizzly bears. They all have a role to play to keep this unique body alive."

Bert asks, "Aren't you just doing that humanizing thing. What do they call it, anthropomorphic? Besides, you sound like one of those Mother Tree believers." As an old-time, ex-timber cutter, Bert isn't quite the believer of the Mother Tree talk that's going around in the forestry world.

In that pastor type of voice, the Pastor says, "You've lived here longer than most people. I know you had to leave for work at times, but you always returned. You can't tell me you don't feel the heart beating here, calling you home."

The Pastor's right about that. There is a place for everyone. You just have to find it, by accident or after much searching.

Bert found his place by accident, coming into the Yaak as a logger during the bark beetle outbreak of the late seventies. He used his wages to buy a small place along the West Fork.

His place.

A timber cutter's world is a mobile world. From the giant firs of Washington and Oregon to the amazing cedars of the Alaska coast, he had cut them all and lived to return to his West Fork retreat. He wouldn't cut another tree for the rest of his days. Even put in a new heat pump so he wouldn't have to cut firewood.

Bert became a planter of trees and a hugger of giant trees. And a lover of this place he calls home.

Eli was right about one thing; this place gets to you. After all Bert's travels for work, he had never seen anything like this place.

Its remoteness, its isolation in winter, and above all, its unique abundance of wildlife and flowing waters.

Bert found his place.

"I tell you," Pastor Eli goes on, "this place is a single living entity. It really doesn't need anything from the outside world. But like any living thing it has health issues."

"And what issues are those?" Bert's more than a little curious.

"People, of course. We are the causes of many of the problems of this unique living landscape. I believe there is a natural balance between everything in this Yaak being. A balance between the wildlife, a balance between the plants, and a balance in our sky-reaching forest. Every piece helping the other pieces. Everything in balance created this unique home of ours. The way I see it, people are the only thing out of balance." He speaks with certainty.

"To be honest," Bert replies, "I'm starting to feel out of balance myself right now after some of your home brew. I got to tell ya, I am not moving outta this place, that's for sure. I like it here, balanced or not."

"But that's the thing. We don't have to be the problem," Eli says. "I firmly believe we could live in this balance too. Humans are smart. We just don't look at all the pieces all the time. We take what we need without thinking how everything is connected to each other.

"If I have learned anything from doing these bathing tours is that people want to believe. They want to believe there is a connection to the natural world that they are missing. They come here with the hope of finding that connection again. They hope what we have here will give them some peace in their lives. Even if it is only for a few minutes. The world of the quiet wild.

"One thing my clients tell me is that they can feel the soul of this place, the heartbeat of this special place. If a place has a soul, a heartbeat, isn't it a living thing?"

"Ya know, Pastor," Bert says, "a lot of folks might think you're a romantic old hippie. Going over the edge, some might say. How about one more brewski before I head home? That's damn good beer."

"You like it?" Eli hands another bottle to Bert. "I use the sugar that's in the cambium layer of our larch trees. Gives it that unique flavor and color. I call it Tall Timber."

They drink in silence for a few minutes.

Finally, Eli says, "People will say what people will say, I can't worry about that. I can only believe in what I believe. What I believe is what's sustaining me. It's what surrounds me here. It's why I wake up every day thankful for being here." His sincerity bleeds through in his words.

"At my age," Bert replies, "half the time, I'm thankful for just waking up. Waking up in this place is the blessing part." He stands, wavering a little. "Well, thanks for the hospitality and the great discussion. Can't wait till next month." He saunters down towards home.

As he walks, he thinks about what Eli had told him. Truth be told, some of what he said made sense. Geographically, the Yaak is surrounded by mountains. Its forest and plant habitat makes it unique. Its varied and abundant wildlife make it like no other part of the state. And the blood thing. The abundance of water in the Yaak originates in this valley's ecosystem.

"Maybe Pastor Eli is onto something in a weird way," Bert mumbles. "Have to think on it."

"Hey, Mister Yaak," Bert shouts, "if you are alive, I'm cool with that. Just don't have your grizzly buddies eat me. Just let me walk home." He chuckles to himself.

It's alive.

The Journey of Pastor Eli will continue.

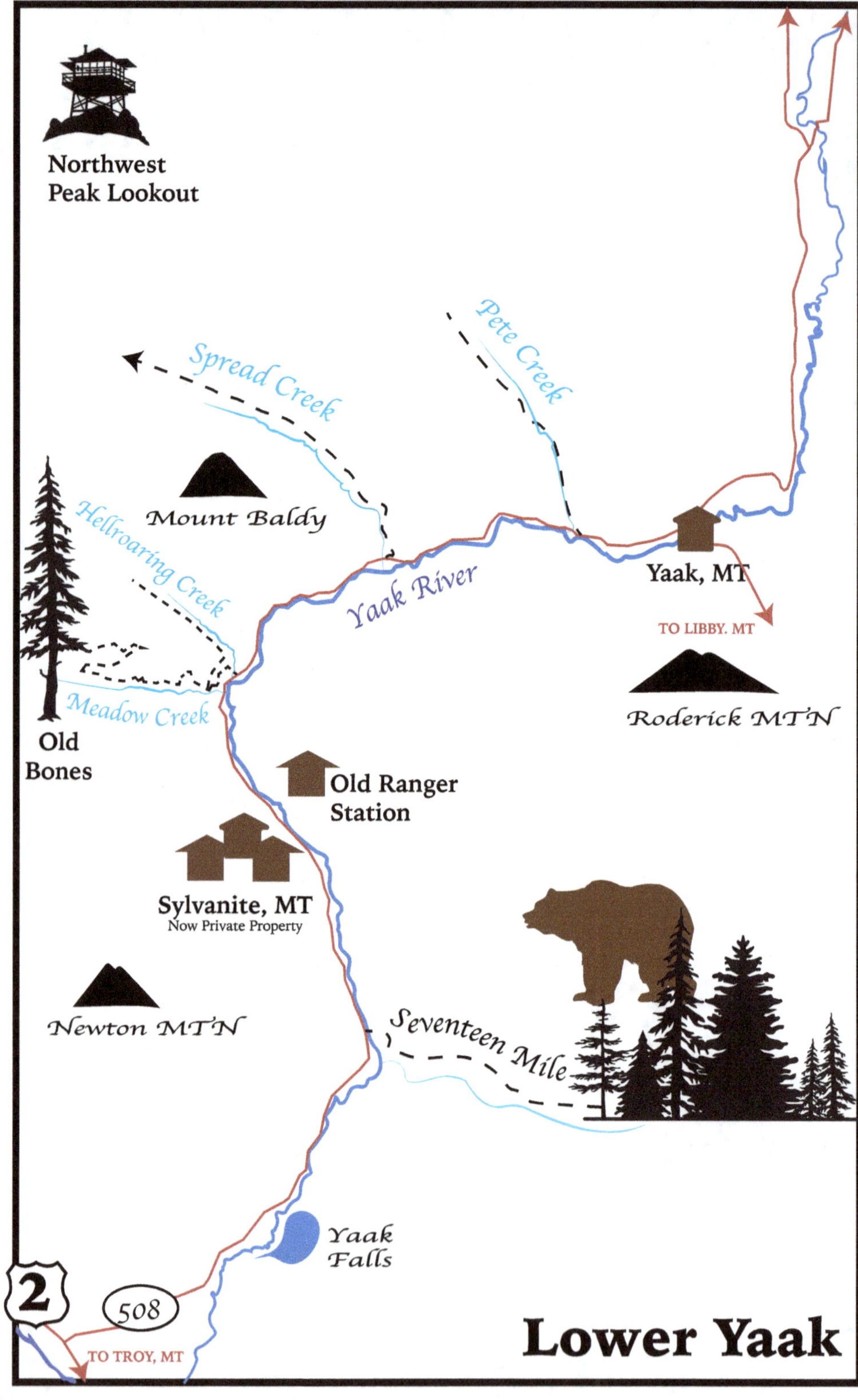

Northwest Peak Lookout
Spread Creek
Pete Creek
Mount Baldy
Hellroaring Creek
Yaak River
Yaak, MT
TO LIBBY. MT
Meadow Creek
Old Bones
Roderick MTN
Old Ranger Station
Sylvanite, MT
Now Private Property
Newton MTN
Seventeen Mile
Yaak Falls
2
508
TO TROY, MT
Lower Yaak

YAAK , Montana

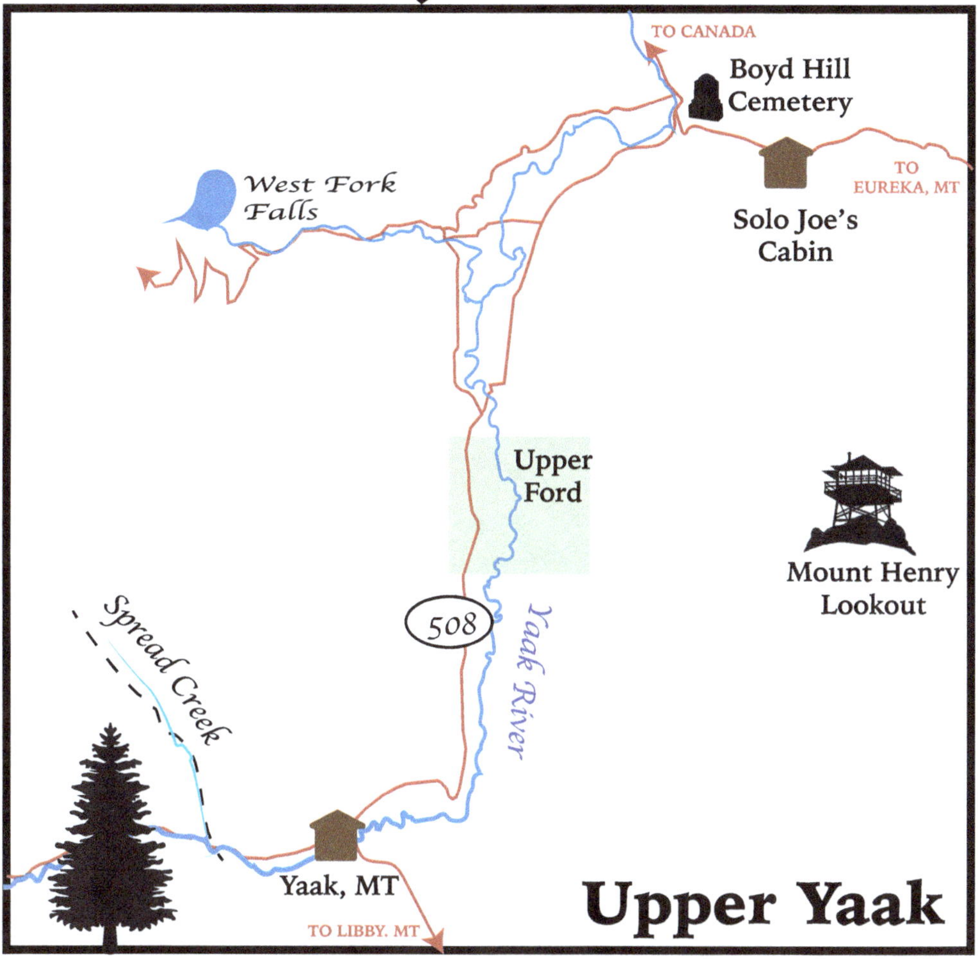

The Homestead

PART TWO: CHAPTER ONE

A Potluck

"You son of a bitch, you haven't said an honest word since you started speaking!" The man interrupts the head of the local environmental group who had started to preach. "Tell the truth or just sit down."

"Please, everyone, just calm down for a minute. This is not a political meeting!" Kathryn the Third, sometimes known to friends and family as Katy Three, tries to hide the nervousness in her voice. "It's just a meet and greet. Please."

The community get-together is not going as she hoped. Hope doesn't always mix well with the real world. Opinions and emotions run strong. Fear of change is even stronger.

The Yaak is changing like never before.

The local timber company decided it's a development company and sold off its river frontage property. Old homesteads have been subdivided. Some are now summer estates. Others are Montana hunting lodges for out-of-state clients.

Some families just want a simple place to park the RV and camp for a few weeks during a Yaak summertime.

Kathryn comes from a long line of Yaak homesteaders. The story is passed down through the family how her grandmother's gift of kindness to a lone caribou led to the gift of the homestead Kathryn now lives on.

Homesteader kindness was at the core of her grandmother Kathryn's beliefs. Help her neighbors when needed. Listen to their stories and complaints. Always be a friend. Living in a remote place like the Yaak, friends can be few and far between.

Kathryn had been born in the Yaak and raised with her grandmother's traditions. She went to the Yaak school and then had to move to Troy for high school, staying with friends during the week. Four years in college in Missoula paid for by her dad's spruce logging business.

Kathryn has long dreamed of returning to that special place. But tonight that dream isn't working out.

"Please, everyone," she implores, "just take some deep breaths for a second."

The idea for the potluck had been born one recent morning during coffee. Her long-time homestead neighbor Patrick had said, "I don't seem to know anyone anymore. Maybe we should just have an old-time potluck and invite anyone interested."

Kathryn added, "I've got a garden full of vegetables that need eating."

Patrick smiled. "I've got a freezer full of elk steaks and a grill that needs using."

"We can meet in my big old empty barn," Kathryn said.

And the potluck was on.

Fliers went up. Anyone and everyone was invited.

Gathered together in her barn, tables laden with food, the arguments begin.

Because, like it or not, life is changing for everyone at the potluck.

Local developers want to increase tourism in the hopes of a big land sale. They dream of Airbnb cabins along the river. RVs are replacing log trucks. Timber beasts eye the last of the big wood. Numerous environmental groups each want to be the savior of the Yaak, their latest place of "special concern." Everyone has ideas how to suck something out of this place Kathryn calls home.

The Yaak keeps giving but it is in need.

What the Yaak needs is Kathryn the Third.

Life has not been easy for the women of her family. Their men die young and early. Grandpa in a logging accident up Pete Creek. Her own father drowned one early morning while casting in the river, doing what he lived for. Two years ago, her contractor husband passed from cancer. The loss strengthened her and made her the woman she was today. Like the world she lives in, Kathryn is a survivor.

Kathryn is also a believer. She believes in living in balance with the wilderness and values what it has given her family over the years. She believes you can have it all. You can have logging that sent her to college. You can have bears in your hills without fear. You can have clean lakes and streams to fish with your family.

She believes in her heart that you can have everything if you're willing to talk.

And listen.

Kathryn knows that to listen is the hardest.

Not much listening going on now.

The Yaak is changing.

New signs are everywhere. Kathryn and the girls call them Yaak daisies.

No Trespassing, Keep Out, Protected by Smith and Wesson and many more scary ones. The girls call them summer pistol packers. None of the old timers with a lifetime of wilderness living ever carried a gun on their hip. These days, whenever she has a beer and a burger at the Tavern, she sees sidearms.

Big money has come into the Yaak and that worries Kathryn. Old homesteads are bought up and subdivided. More signs going up, more areas closed down. Kathryn has received offers for unbelievable amounts of money for her family holdings, more than she ever imagined.

Buy a nice condo in Vegas, they say.

They're funny. They don't know the Yaak or its people.

Yaak homesteaders die here. Many are buried in family cemeteries.

In the beginning, Kathryn had even joined one environmental group because she was impressed with their community work and the good they claimed to be doing for the Yaak.

Soon she realized their idea of good was chasing big eastern money to pay eastern writers to write about saving the Yaak and to fund big lawsuits. The locals didn't matter to them.

Kathryn believes in a working, living Yaak. She believes in a Yaak with open trails to the high mountain lakes.

Kathryn believes in good. A believer in people and the good they can bring into the Yaak. A shining new church to gather in. A quilting club. A new fire hall with dedicated volunteers. A tavern to get a darn good burger and cold beer with neighbors. Music along the river.

Kathryn rings the old dinner bell to quiet the crowd. "Please everyone, calm down a little. Let's rest our opinions a bit and eat some of this great food you all have brought. Please dig in."

Grumbling fades as people fill their plates and move to folding tables and chairs.

Food is a great healer. Her mom taught her long ago you can't yell with your mouth full.

Potlucks used to be a way of life in the Yaak. You never know what you're going to get. All salads one time, all desserts the next. That's the fun and mystery of potlucks.

Some foods are the best you've ever eaten, others not so much. Some is strange—that's the mystery part.

Most is delicious. Venison and elk smokies, elk steaks, homemade bread, hand-churned ice cream and huckleberry pies. Even dandelion wine and maybe a little moonshine.

As people enjoy the great mix of food, tempers ease. Laughter creeps in.

Kathryn watches and realizes her changing world is like a potluck.

Like what's going on now in the Yaak. A mix of everything and you never know what changes are coming your way.

Some want to sell every inch of the Yaak. Others want to lock up every inch. Some changes are sweet, and some are bitter. Many people just want to be left alone.

Maybe breaking bread at a potluck with friends, strangers, and neighbors is a good start.

And at a potluck, one thing appeals to everyone—great homemade dessert.

Maybe the Yaak is the dessert we all crave.

PART TWO: CHAPTER TWO

Early Morning Cast

Can we really leave it to beaver?

Swissssssssssssh. The fly line sweeps across the still-early morning waters with that special dry fly. As the leader unrolls, the fly lands exactly where Kathryn wants it to be, where it's supposed to be. The brown fly gently floats under overhanging brush of her new beaver pond.

Kathryn's father loved to take his daughter fishing as much as possible. Owning a long stretch of the Yaak River didn't hurt. But, in addition to fun, living on the homestead required endless chores, like animals to tend to and firewood to haul. Dad and Mom had worked hard every day to feed and clothe their little family.

Homestead work was never done but fishing time made Yaak life perfect, and her dad made sure their lives were perfect. And he taught her well. With all the burden of a true fisher person.

She always cherished her father's desire to be on the river at daybreak. To take her to the river then. Their special time.

That early morning cast. The joy of watching the river world come alive. Early morning is wildlife time. There is a special bonding between river and fisher person in that morning reflective light. Everything is new and fresh. A time to think. A time to be at peace with her world. The river drinkers, the fish hunters. Her father taught all their names and how to respect their world.

The early morning sun light is starting to peek through the old growth larch along the edge of the pond when the strike hits. Fast, hard, and gone. That's fishing. Kathryn smiles and casts again with a slow leader roll. Hard to believe that, not too long ago, this beautiful pond was a cow wallow.

"Beavers," she mutters. "First, we killed them off now we are bringing them back."

With a flip of his head, a Belted Kingfisher downs a small fish. That tells Kathryn he appreciates the new fishing hole. "Glad you like it," she says.

Wham! Another fish strikes. Not losing this puppy. She nets a 14-inch rainbow trout. Then she releases it back into the pond.

Beavers. Who would have guessed the difference they'd make?

It began with her daughter's idea for a school project. She had learned in the Yaak school that beavers were helping to restore damaged wetlands.

Can we do this? She'd asked Kathryn.

Living in the land of beaver trappers, Kathryn didn't know how to answer. A lot of her neighbors, whom she liked, trapped beavers for various reasons.

As a fly fisher, sure, the more beaver ponds the better. Beaver ponds are mystic words to fisher people—places where fish have never been fished, where cutthroat trout never stop. Like the rainbow ponds at Smoot Creek. The legendary cutthroat ponds of upper Seventeen Mile Creek.

But beavers were in trouble. Over-trapping, disease, loss of habitat were various reasons. Some of Kathryn's favorite fishing ponds had no beavers and had collapsed.

The Yaak was changing.

When Kathryn and her family had returned to take over the family homestead, they'd known they were home forever. Two years ago, her husband died from cancer and was buried on the family cemetery. Forever became real. The pain of his loss was real, but the love of family is more real. Like the Yaak, she survives.

Another perfect cast and a slow drift. A couple of beavers made that possible.

Owning one of the biggest spreads in the Yaak means endless work. Kathryn had learned long ago that the day never ends, and you are forever chasing something. Life on the homestead never stops.

Hard work is the life she's chosen and, after losing her partner, she cherishes it every day more than ever.

But she needs peaceful time, too. That time for herself. That walk-with-the-dog time. That time to ponder.

That early morning river time. That first cast time.

Yaak River near Pete Creek.

But the homestead needed help. Overgrazing, streams that had been trampled. Land in the Yaak has been used hard.

Land rich is one thing, but money rich is another. Kathryn is not money rich. The occasional timber sale, pasture leases, hay sales and the local farmers market are her livelihood.

No lack of offers from the bank to borrow on the ranch. No lack of conservation groups telling her what's best. No lack of suitors telling her she needs help. But those choices would be the end of her freedom as she knows it.

Maybe someday.

Kathryn wants her girls to go to college and have a great life. She wants to make a living off the ranch without gutting it. She needs a plan. She knows she needs help.

Wham! Another strike. Another nice fish. Glad she tied that floater after all. Better make these beavers a special gift of saplings for dinner.

So, with supervision from her girls, she researched beavers. The animals were hurting but making a comeback.

Beaver support groups would help transport and transplant beavers for free. This might work, she'd thought.

She owned the wetlands but any creatures that made it to the river were fair game to trapping.

With no money to build earthen dams, she and the girls got to work with shovels and sticks. After a time, the pond became wide enough and started filling. Now they hoped, the beavers themselves could finish the rest.

The beaver people brought two pairs and released them in two different creek areas of the ranch. The sound of running water is too much for beavers. So, build they did. Like crazy.

Pretty soon, the ponds formed, and a variety of bird life moved in. So did the fish. Her daughters put signs along the river that read: "Leave our beavers please."

Only time will tell if beavers survive. Funny how people like seeing beavers being gutted on TV.

As the sun crests the old growth, Kathryn must head back for never-ending chores. The early morning gossip of geese greets her as she hikes along the river. The hello of a blue heron makes her smile.

A whiff of the smoke from the homestead says she is home. Her Yaak is starting to heal. One simple step at a time. One morning cast at a time.

One plan at a time.

The Plan

"Mommy," little Aspen Rose screams.

Like a human gazelle, Kathryn races through the river boulders to her youngest daughter.

Her daughter stands frozen in time by the river.

"Aspen, what's wrong?" Kathryn yells.

"There's caca on the beach again, Mommy," Aspen says. "It's gross, Mommy."

"Well, step away and I'll get a stick to bury it." Kathryn mutters. "Damn rafters."

As Kathryn buries the offending matter, she continues to mumble, "What in the hell was the state thinking when they thought bringing in more tourists would be great. Tourists without toilets."

Toilet paper is becoming the new Montana state flower. They bloom everywhere. Forest Service trailheads, pullouts, river access sites, and even private property.

That's how tourists are—poop today, gone tomorrow.

No worries, let the locals take care of it. Let's get back on the river!

Enough. It's time to get ready for her hike with her ladies hiking group. Hips and Lips they secretly call them themselves. Keep the hips moving and chatting helps the trail go by.

Today's trip is to Mt. Henry lookout for a great view. Fun, but also kind of sad. All her hiking ladies are widows including herself. It seems the Yaak is hard on men.

Some died in logging accidents, some drowned fishing the Yaak, and many like Kathryn's partner passed from the cancer. Life can be cruel, but women still hug and dance. The strength they gain in their loss brings them together to share strength with each other. They are her support group, hiking group, but most of all they are her dancing sisters.

Like the Yaak, they are survivors.

As they turn off the Yaak road and head up the Solo Joe Road, Kathryn remembers when her father told her about old Solo Joe and his life in the Yaak. As one of the first homesteaders, Solo wanted to be left alone to wander his East Fork claims. The neighbors had to take him away from his homestead when he couldn't care for himself anymore. He died a short time later in the old folk's home. A homesteader without a homestead.

Kathryn always finds solace and laughter in her memories. Like going 23 miles downriver with her dad for gas to Gene and Ruthie Grush's, the first place to have electricity in the Yaak. With power, Gene installed a gas pump and Ruthie put in a new electric stove and blender. Kathryn loved it when Gene told his tales with a sparkle in his eyes as she nibbled a fresh oven treat baked by Ruthie.

One favorite story was the time John McIntire got Gene so drunk on John's moonshine whiskey that he puked on their wood cook stove. Gene would have fallen face first into it if Dirty Sally, Jeannette Nolan's stage name, hadn't caught him. Gene always related that story with his great laugh and a wink.

The women reach the parking lot. As they head up the trail to the lookout, Kathryn hangs back. She likes to go last to give her time to think. She has lots to ponder.

The Plan.

After a family meeting, she and the girls decided they needed to get proactive in their little world.

They're going into the tourist trade. Like it or not, tourists are here. The family cashed in some inheritance money and had three Yurts put in along the river for bird watchers. Kathryn's mother had been a fanatic birder and taught her many names. She also taught her about the money involved with birders.

Kathryn had even met with local wildlife and ecology experts to talk about leading nature hikes on the ranch.

Nature healing. Nature to heal a troubled soul.

When Kathryn first explored the business idea, she had to laugh. Nature was her place in the world, the reason some people live in the Yaak. She'd never seen it as a business. Funny new world.

When she was little and sassed her mom, her mother used to tell her, "Take it to the river stump. Really not interested right now."

Kathryn had indeed found a special stump. Right by the river, a spruce stump from a tree that was now part of the lumber of their home. One of Montana's rarest flowers surrounded the stump, the Yaaks Tiger Lily, found only in the Yaak. The stump was protected by her old-growth cedar friend with its black bear hangout. There, Kathryn had shared many frustrations, arguments, and private tears for the loss of her parents and partner.

The nature of the Yaak had always helped her soul. Maybe it could help others. Gave her something to think about.

As the hikers reach the summit of Mt. Henry, they sigh at the amazing views of Caribou Mountain and Canada to the north, Glacier Park to the east, and Northwest Peak to the west.

But the condition of the abandoned lookout saddens Kathryn.

After lunch, the women hold a simple ceremony of remembrance for Shamus, the guardian who for years had protected the upper Yaak from this high perch. Her father always said he slept better on those hot summer nights knowing Shamus was watching over them. During his career, Shamus spotted many a fire and helped guide many a firefighter.

Shamus is gone and the Yaak is changing.

The women laugh and clang hiking poles on rocks as they head down the mountain, looking forward to burgers and cold beer at the local tavern.

Kathryn worries about the Yaak's future. For the first time, hate is showing up. Graffiti bothers her the most—political statements and childish vandalism.

She misses little things like the Yaak road wave. Not an index finger wave but a stick-your-whole-hand-out-the-window kind of wave. Pretty good chance you recognized who you were waving at.

Kathryn still ponders about the future of the ranch. The hayfields will stay for now. Hay pays the bills.

The loss of grazing leases hurts financially but the pastures need a rest. They've been overgrazed for years and are now covered in weeds.

She even reached out to a local environmental group that has given advice to other homesteads. Her complaints to her Forest Service neighbors about weeds along the joint property lines go nowhere. No management plan for that, they say.

The Forest Service.

Over the years, her father wasn't fond of dealing with the Forest Service. Called them "Two and Done Foresters". Young tree-struck foresters show up in the Yaak for a couple of years. They recite catch phrases like forest restoration, shelter wood cuts, and now fuel reduction. Millions of board feet of timber get punched on their resume. Then they move on before anyone sees what they did. If her dad were alive today, he would compare them to tourists who poop in the woods and leave before someone sees it.

Kathryn is not her father. She enjoys her dealings with the

Forest Service. She enjoys many cold beers at the Tavern with them. Some current foresters were born in the Yaak and they have a special place in her heart. She knows they're trying to do what's best for the Yaak.

But decisions come from faraway worlds no one understands.

Many locals don't think about the fact that every Forest Service employee has to answer to over three hundred million Americans, all of whom have a right to their opinion. Kathryn hates having even one boss, let alone three hundred million. Not an easy place to be.

But she has concerns about proposed logging along the north end and if it will affect her new beaver ponds.

At the Tavern, the women finish their darned good burgers and a couple of beers. Time for hugs all around to finish the day.

Kathryn's days are never finished. At times, she barely keeps up. The first Yurt guests arrive this weekend, a website designer and his family. She bartered a weekend of camping for him in exchange for his work setting up her website. Her pop taught her to never give away a dollar bill when you can barter instead.

She needs to help Aspen Rose put up her new signs along the river. They say, "Don't poop in my yard please."

One hug at a time.

One plan at a time.

One day at a time, it's all you can do really.

A side note. The life of Gene Grush is well documented in the History of the Forest Service in the Yaak. What is not documented his Gene's love of a good tale. I still remember sitting on my truck tailgate getting gas and listening to Gene spin his yarns. I just wish I could remember them all. Sad to say I was there that early morning when they lost their beautiful home to a simple chimney fire. They just stood there holding each other. They survived and rebuilt. Survivors like the Yaak, they lived on.

They lived on in my memories too.

PART TWO: CHAPTER FOUR

A Wounded Pony

A wounded pony.
A wounded heart.
A confused Grizzly Bear.

Elk butts.
The eternal question.
Kathryn the Third drank her second coffee and wondered why some elk butts are white and some are brown.

The elk were grazing on the first green grass in the lower pasture in the mist of the Yaak River in that special early morning light. This was common on the ranch in the spring, but still every time she had coffee with her elk buddies it felt special. Like the first time her dad introduced her to the elk on the ranch in the spring. The importance of letting them be. Spring is their time. A time to heal from a long winter. A time to give birth in safety.

Her parents believed in the balance of nature. Give the elk feed and safety in the spring and you might get a little winter's meat in the fall. You can reap the balance of the wilderness if you understand that balance. Take only what you need. And share what you have. They taught her it will always come back as a blessing.

But something was wrong in the elk herd on this misty morning. One of the elk was not looking right. Too much red.

A quick scan with the spotting scope, Kathryn saw it was not an elk but a very wounded horse. "WTF? I don't have any horses," she mumbled.

The first thing, she called her longtime homestead neighbor Patrick. He had horses and used to have the Forest Service contract to pack supplies to the lookouts in the Yaak.

"Lose a horse, Patrick?" Kathryn asked. "I got one in my lower pasture that's looking pretty sad."

"I haven't had any stock in a few years," Patrick said.

"Patrick, I haven't been around much horse stock. Not sure what I should do. Would you help me out?"

"Let me make some calls about a missing horse, then I'll be over."

As Kathryn watched the elk move on, the sad horse didn't take a step. Just stood there waiting to die, she thought.

When Patrick arrived, he said, "That's one hurting horse for sure. Made some calls and no one is missing a beat-up pony. But I heard about a couple of cowboys who were drinking at the Strip. They were trying to ride to Alaska. Said they had a horse that just gave up. Said he was only worth grizzly bait."

Patrick went on to explain the horse had been bought at an auction in southern Idaho by a couple of "Rendezvous wannabes," dudes who wanted to relive the 1880s. They put a bad-fitting pack saddle on him and treated him as nothing more than a piece of meat. As they worked their way north, the pack saddle dug into his flesh. Constant whipping left wounds on his flanks.

As the back-to-1880s types started working their way through the blow down of the Yaak, the horse could go no farther. He just gave up. No matter how much they whipped him and cursed him he had no interest in moving. He was done.

They decided to cut him loose and leave him, alone and hurt, in the wilderness. Grizzly bait.

"This is one hurting horse." Patrick said again as he surveyed the poor pony. Flies had been busy in the wounds left by the pack saddle. Cuts on his flanks and legs showed the whip marks. "How can someone who calls themselves horse people do this?"

He faced Kathryn. "This little guy needs a lot of help. Not sure if you want to do what's needed. There's a Canadian horse buyer roaming around. Probably give you a hundred bucks for him."

Kathryn pulled herself up to her full height. "This horse is not going to France to be hamburger, I'll tell you that."

All her longtime neighbor homesteaders knew about Kathryn's family history of compassion, of being there when needed. Of her grandmother saving a caribou. Of her mom's potlucks to bring people together, a tradition Kathryn had continued. The strength of raising two daughters and running a ranch alone.

She made the decision. "I have to help this poor guy somehow."

"This is not going to be easy," Patrick said. "I'll be here for you, but we need to move him to the barn. Get him out of the flies."

The horse would not move. After Patrick put a halter on him, he still wouldn't move. He was beaten, worn out, past caring. He was done.

A simple touch changed everything.

Kathryn and Patrick were still standing with the lost horse when her daughters Eleanor Star and Aspen Rose came running up the driveway after school.

"We have a horse?" They yelled in unison.

"Hold on, girls," Kathryn said. "Not sure that we have. Found him in the pasture this morning. He's in bad shape, needs help, and won't move. I'm not sure what to do."

Her oldest, Elly Star, spoke with a seriousness Kathryn had never heard before. "What we do, Mommy, is help."

Little Aspen added, "It's what we do, Mommy. It's what our family has always done. It's us."

Their understanding surprised Kathryn.

Then it happened.

The wounded soul lowered his head. Little hands of innocent love scratched horse's ears that had never been touched in kindness, had never known love.

A simple touch.

When is a horse-crazy girl born? Maybe when the large heart of a hurt pony finds its way into the large hearts of two little girls.

"Can we keep him?" Both girls asked.

"Not sure," Kathryn said. "But if we can, first we need to get him in the barn and clean his wounds."

"We'll call him Huckleberry," Aspen said.

"Yes, Huckleberry," Elly agreed.

And the horse now called Huckleberry maybe felt hopeful for the first time.

The long family tradition of carrying for wounded souls began again. Cuts were cleaned. Salves were applied. Love was given through the touch of young hands.

Kathryn talked with Jacob the Sheriff who said, "If no one claims the horse in thirty days, it's yours. To be honest, if someone does show up to claim that horse, I'm going to arrest his butt for animal abuse." He shook his head. "If you can save it, I'm pretty sure it's yours."

As Kathryn watched her girls bond with Huckleberry, she saw the emptiness in their little hearts being filled for the first time since their father's loss. The little horse needed them, but they needed him more. Funny how things are meant to be.

Huckleberry was healing. Kathryn hoped for healing in her Yaak world.

***

Shoot, Shovel, and Shut Up is once again the theme song for the Yaak. Grizzlies in the Yaak have long faced the three SSS's.

This time, a female grizzly and cubs were brutally slaughtered just for their paws.

Generations of Kathryn's family always lived fine with the bears in their world. Or was it them in the bears' world? Wolves and grizzlies are an important part of the wilderness balance.

Kathryn still remembers the early 1980s when she witnessed the first grizzly bear transplanted to the Sylvanite Ranger Station.

Two weeks later, its collar had been cut off and was found under the bridge on the East Fork of the Yaak River. Funny how the collar still worked under water.

Shoot, Drowned, Shut Up.

Then there was the guy who killed a grizzly with two cubs feeding on his hanging deer.

Because the Yaak is more Rocky Mountain boulders than dirt, shoveling is not an option. He built a monster wood slash pile and tried burning them up. Funny, the tracking collars still beeped even when burned.

Shoot. Burn. Shut Up.

The latest local grizzly bear meeting is even more confusing with so many voices. The Forest Service, federal bear folks, environmental groups, Native Americans, the Border Patrol, and of course the lawyers. Lots of lawyers.

The Forest Service claims logging will help the grizzlies with better food sources.

The local Ktunaxa Tribe claims logging will return the land to its natural state.

The environmental groups claim there are only 25 struggling, starved bears in the recovery area.

The federal bear people claim there could be up to 50 to 60 grizzlies in the recovery zone.

The Border Patrol claim new logging roads will lead to hordes of immigrants crossing.

The Forest Service won't hold meetings away from the district office because of the verbal political assault they now face.

Lawyers have taken over the Yaak. Want to cut a tree? Call a lawyer. Want to save a tree? Call a lawyer. Want to hike a Yaak trail? Check with a lawyer. Don't like your new out-of-state neighbors? Call a lawyer.

Lawyers seem to be the only ones making money in the Yaak these days.

Kathryn hears many voices speaking for the Yaak these days.

There is one voice that will never be heard in a court of law. The voice of the Yaak. The voice of its streams and creeks. The voice of wind blowing through the trees. The voice of that special silence on a winter's morning. This is the voice Kathryn hears.

The Yaak is off balance for sure but not gone. Kathryn knows life in the Yaak wilderness brings the best out of people who never knew what they could do. Remoteness and long winters bring out a strength in people when it is needed the most.

The voice of survival is strong in the Yaak. The survival of the bears, the wolves, and all its special critters. Of the people. And even a wounded pony. Without these survivors there is no Yaak. Just another suburbanite's world.

***

As Kathryn watches her daughters spoil Huckleberry with grain and a new horse blanket from neighbor Patrick, she knows, at the end of the day, there's always hope.

You never know what might be found in that mist-covered pasture with the next Yaak sunrise.

PART TWO: CHAPTER 5
Life with Bears

"Griz in the pasture, Mom," Elly Star says looking out the window.

"Where's Aspen Rose?" Kathryn asks, thinking of her little wild child who likes to roam. At that instant, she sees her youngest daughter on the deck.

And something else is beyond, out in the pasture.

Famous Amos, their new rescue dog, is mousing in the grass, just like the grizzly bear, right behind him.

"Aspen, hurry, call your dog!" Kathryn yells.

When Aspen calls Amos's name, he comes running without hesitation. He never sees the bruin behind him.

But Aspen's voice causes the bear to raise its head. It makes a quick right turn up the hill and disappears into the timber.

Man, Kathryn thinks, they can run fast when they want to.

Aspen and Amos. Funny how those two bonded instantly. A child named after a wild rose was bound to have a little wild streak. No surprise she'd like a dog with a major wild streak.

Famous Amos, they named him. Born on a Montana

reservation. Running wild with no parents or siblings. Never taught any dog manners. Just running scared. A local rescue shelter picked him up before he was shot.

Kathryn and the girls had stopped at the local shelter to donate straw. Before you know it, there's Aspen playing with her new buddy. The people at the shelter warned he was a real wild one and would be hard to train.

The family had been talking about getting a dog for a while. Might help with the influx of bears.

From the way the girls were hugging him, Kathryn knew they had their new dog.

He was young and ill-mannered but with the faith of two young girls he became a member of the pack.

That's the second grizzly they've seen on the ranch this spring. The third in two years. That's more than Kathryn saw as a child growing up.

The last couple of years, black bears are frequent, returning from the previous year along with new ones. Mild winters and good berries help their population. The girls give them nicknames like Pie Face, Limby, and Big Fatty.

***

In the old days in the Yaak, if you saw a bear, the custom was Shoot, shovel, shut up.

In past times, Kathryn's father killed his share of black bears on the ranch. Sold the hide and fed his family.

Kathryn's mom wouldn't cook the meat or eat it. She liked the bears alive. She believed what the local Ktunaxa people believed. *k'waya' were the great spirit gift to Mother Earth. They were considered sacred beings, honored for their strength and cunning. They were seen as guardians of the people by the way they protected their cubs. Native people did not kill their protectors.

The Yaak has bears, both grizzly and black. The Pacific Northwest habitat provides plenty of water and bear food. Huckleberries, service berries, wild strawberries, choke cherries, elder berries, Glacier lilies. Don't forget the ants. Bears love ants.

The Yaak has so many bears that hunting magazines in the southwest publicize that. Need that bear hide for your weekend cabin in the hills? Go to the Yaak.

Every spring in the seventies and early eighties, hordes of bear hunters showed up like the cavalry to massacre young bears. They drove around on three-wheelers and in pickups with seats mounted in the back so they could shoot anything that moved.

Not good for the bears.

In spring, all bears, young and old, black and grizzly, need fresh grass to get their digestive track working after a long winter's hibernation. The first green grass grows on hillsides along roads.

They became easy targets for these road-roaming hunters. A lot of young bears died not for the meat but for that hide to hang as decoration in that cabin.

Kathryn still remembers seeing the carcasses of small bears dumped in local trash green boxes. It struck her how freaking weird that a small skinned-out bear looks like a little human. Depressing that young bear's life is a piece of trash to some people.

Thankfully the Forest Service and the grizzly bear guardians saw the wisdom of protecting the critters by closing off many roads in the spring. This simple but important act has rewritten bear survival for years to come.

Many of Kathryn's neighbors still hunt bears. You can buy a tag that allows you to hunt deer, elk, and black bear. That's a lot of meat. One neighbor claims to have killed more than 35 bears. Says they are easy to kill. Most times, they just roll over and die.

Kathryn's worst memories were circus bear hunters who showed up in spring to hunt females with cubs. They killed the mom and captured the crying cubs to train for circus shows. Those cute bears riding a barrel had to come from somewhere. Somewhere was often the Yaak.

But grizzlies in the pasture are something else altogether. Kathryn even broke out her father's old shotgun, cleaned it, and shot a few rounds to get used to it. She didn't plan to kill but to make noise.

This grizzly thing confuses her more all the time. Some claim there are only a few remaining grizzlies in the Yaak. If that's so, she asks herself, why are grizzlies showing up in my yard? Just over the hill in northern Idaho, bears moving there and eating pigs. She wonders, are there more people in bear country or just more bears?

Another thing that confuses her is the hate and fear many new folks feel about the bears. They must have watched Night of the Grizzlies too many times.

At the tavern, she sees guns on the hips of people who think that will make them safe.

Maybe they don't know what happened with the two out-of-state black bear hunters on Northwest Peak. One hunter tangled with a female grizzly and a cub eating huckleberries. His partner decided it was best to shoot the bear. He shot and wounded the female but he also shot and killed his partner. Others had to hunt down and kill the wounded female and cub. Sad all around.

Hunters on Indian and Chief Mountain killed a young male

they thought was following them. Fear runs strong and you never know about grizzly bears.

When Kathryn and family returned to the ranch, one of the first chores was restore the garden. She wanted to grow as much of their own food as possible. They replaced a funky deer fence and added a 6000-volt electric bear fence. The manufacturer claimed it was designed to stop water buffaloes and grizzly bears. She already had grizzlies but you never know when water buffaloes might show up.

Because many critters cross the big ranch property, Kathryn is working with local federal grizzly people on ways to avoid conflict. They identify game corridors where bears are most likely to travel. They work to limit disruption in those areas by limiting food sources. No garbage allowed out at her new Yurt rentals. Keep feed contained for Huckleberry the pony. The feds even loaned her an electric mat to place near the chicken coop.

Bear spray by the door.

Growing up, black bears never really bothered Kathryn, but now, every spring there seem to be more. They used to run in fear when they saw humans. Now they swim in the pond in the front yard. Funny in a way, Kathryn thinks. They act more like neighbors than wild critters.

Grizzlies add a whole new dimension to the story. You might call them the kings of the Yaak jungle. They're always hungry.

Nowadays, anytime Kathryn walks away from the house, she straps on a can of bear spray.

She still laughs when she remembers showing her daughters how it worked. They wanted to spray each other. Thankfully she stopped them before they turned into spicy tacos.

She's relieved the grizzly in the pasture that morning didn't bother Famous Amos but instead ran away into the timber.

The grizzly debate never ends. Hate them. Fear them. Kill them. Love them. Live with them. Whatever one thinks about them, they somehow survive like the children of Three Paws of Pete Creek Meadows or the estimated fifty-eight bloodline children of the legendary DJ of Seventeen Mile Creek. Bears, black and grizzly, are the story of the Yaak.

Like the Yaak, their children survive.

When we are gone, they will survive.

PART TWO: CHAPTER SIX

Aspen Leaves

"Story time, story time!" The girls screamed in unison as they jumped into bed that winter evening.

"And what story are we going to tell tonight?" Kathryn asked, already knowing the answer.

"We want a tree story, how Aspen got her name." Little Elly snuggles under the warm comforter.

Between modern toys like computers and the endless junk on satellite television, one thing that was a constant in Kathryn's world was winter story time. Summers were always too busy around the ranch with endless chores, leaving no time for stories.

But when Yaak winter snow settled around the warm cabin and things slowed down, nights became the perfect time for books by the fire and bedside stories. When Kathryn was young, her mother always read to her, and she enjoyed telling a tall tale or two. Kathryn made sure the stories in her family were kept alive.

Stories about one tree or another had been part of her family for as long as she could remember.

She settled on the bed between the two girls, an arm around

each. "Well, it all begins with Mother Nature and her love of this special place called the Yaak. When Momma Nature was done decorating the world with her beautiful things, she saved the best for her favorite place. She gave this place special gifts. That's why our home has so many beautiful different trees, flowers, and animals."

"And aspen trees," Little Aspen Rose added with a laugh.

"And aspen trees of course," Kathryn agreed with a smile. "Mother Nature gave so many different types of trees to the Yaak it's hard to remember them all. But one tree was special because she had only a few left and each one carried a small part of herself. So, she scattered them across the meadows and open fields along the river.

"You see, each grove of aspen was given its own mother tree. The gift of Mother Nature. Unlike most trees that start from seed, children grow from the roots of a mother aspen tree. They will forever be connected as one family with a loving mother. She will raise them and nurture them to become a beautiful stand of aspen trees. Our Native American friends believe aspen groves mean family and togetherness."

"Like us, right, Mommy?" Daughter Elizabeth Star chimed in.

Kathryn laughed. "You're not a tree, but we will always be family."

Elizabeth Star snuggled deeper under the comforter.

Kathryn went on, "The morning we brought little Aspen home from the hospital we hadn't picked a name yet, so Daddy and I went and sat in our aspen grove to think of one. As we sat there, red aspen leaves came dancing down on the breeze all around us. Soon a carpet of red leaves covered the ground. This only happens once and a while, and no one knows when. So of course, we named you Aspen because the mother aspen blessed you that day with a special gift of leaves of color."

Aspen Rose's eyes had grown heavy with sleep as she mumbled,

Rare red aspen leaves.

"My birthday present."

***

Tree scientists consider aspen leaves turning red a rare phenomenon. Three things must come together in nature's harmony for this to happen. Rainfall at the perfect time and amount. Warm fall days and cool nights with no frost. And a little thing called genes. It could happen only once or over and over. There's no way to predict. In all the years we've lived here, 2022 is the first time we have seen it in our trees.

The most massive living organism known on planet earth is a single aspen grove in Utah estimated to be 14,000 years old. I've had lunch there and it's impressive for sure. Lots of yellow.

I'd like to be there in the year of red leaves.

PART TWO: CHAPTER 7

A Simple Tree

"Mommy, it's getting late. Do you think he's okay?" Little Aspen Rose's brows furrow with worry.

Elizabeth Star also stares out the window, frowning. "He never forgot us before."

"I'm sure he's okay and hasn't forgotten you two. Remember, Patrick isn't young anymore and moves a lot slower these days." Kathryn tries to sound cheerful. "He'll be here soon."

When she'd talked to him last weekend, he said he would be here like always on the morning of December 22nd with the tree. He said he had a special tree in mind but needed to take a snowshoe trip to get it. He sounded excited about a nice winter adventure.

***

Before Kathryn's husband died, when the girls were little, every December 22nd, their dad would go out that morning on snowshoes. He cut down their Christmas tree and snowshoed back through the pasture, hauling the tree. The girls watched from the house barely able to contain their excitement.

Then cancer took him from them.

Their longtime homestead neighbor and friend, Patrick, knew the first Christmas without a husband and father in the house was going to be a rough one. He had recently lost his wife. Knowing how hard it was on a grown man, he couldn't imagine how two little girls and a new widow would feel.

He was not a rich man, but he did what he could. He decided to cut a simple Christmas tree for them. One less thing to worry about. The tradition was born.

Every year since, on December 22nd, he snowshoed out and brought the girls a special tree.

But this morning is December 22nd and no sign of him. Kathryn tries calling a couple of times, but he rarely picks up the phone because of junk calls. No caller ID for him.

"I'm going to drive over and check on him," she tells her daughters. "You girls go feed Huckleberry."

At Patrick's homestead, she finds the place eerily quiet. She calls for him. Nothing. Two days of snow but no fresh tracks nor signs of shoveling. Inside the house, the wood stove has not been lit in a couple of days.

Memories of her grandfather and father, dying alone in Yaak wilderness, come back to Kathryn, along with those of her husband's last struggle with cancer. Patrick has cancer, too.

She hurries home to make phone calls.

***

Patrick had been a natural wanderer. It seemed wandering was in his blood. In his young life, with no thought to his future, he wandered from one place to the next. One day he wandered into a place called the Yaak and found an old homestead. He bought it with the little savings he had.

Then he met another wanderer.

For more than 40 years, they shared a life of homesteading, but continued to wander to the high mountain lakes to fish.

Patrick had the Forest Service contract to supply the fire lookouts in the Yaak. Mount Henry, Caribou Mountain, Mount Baldy, and Northwest Peak were his world, and he loved every minute. He wandered high mountain trails and always enjoyed meeting the young lookout people. In all those years, he never missed a delivery date.

The lookouts were eventually abandoned and there were no more contracts. After 43 years of blissful marriage, his reason for living passed. He still had friends among the old homestead families, but fewer and fewer were left. Boyd Hill Cemetery was filling up with his friends.

Others sold out to developers. He didn't know his new neighbors. "They drive too fast," he said.

Kathryn and the girls made sure he was part of their family with regular invites to Sunday dinner. The girls rode their old horse Huckleberry to his place, using the excuse to deliver cookies and brownies, but he knew they really came to check on him.

During his summer wandering, he scouted out the Christmas tree he planned to deliver to the family on December 22nd.

Old age, the loss of his longtime partner, the loneliness of cancer and the treatments sapped his energy and sometimes left him depressed.

"But not at Christmas time, by god." His girls needed their tree, and that delivery gave him a reason to care again.

His snowshoe days were coming to an end so this year it must be a special tree. He had found the tree he wanted. Not a spruce or Doug fir. Not a white pine or yellow pine. But a perfectly shaped grand fir with the best smell of any tree.

It grew a few miles from his home, not on any trail. That was a problem because it meant a bushwhack snowshoe trip. But if this was his last tree run, he might as well make it worthwhile. It had to be this tree.

On the morning of the 21st, Christmas tree permit in hand,

Patrick headed out. He took enough food and water for three days. Experience taught him you never know what can happen in the wilderness.

He figured he'd spend most of that day getting to the destination, cut the tree, and camp on the way back. He'd return in time to show up the morning of the 22nd like always.

He loved this winter world. Studying the fresh animal tracks. Enjoying the sound of solitude on a winter's trail.

At the beginning of the day, breaking trail came easy. There's an art to wearing snowshoes and Patrick was skilled after many years of winter trapping. At first, the going was invigorating and brought back good memories.

Soon the snow grew deeper. He didn't remember this much blown-down timber. His pace slowed but remained steady. "One step and then another," he kept telling himself. As the day wore on, the snow came up to his knees and his energy faded, but he could not stop yet.

As the light waned into darkness, he reached the tree. Covered with fresh snow, it looked perfect.

Too tired to continue, he decided to make camp. In the stub of a burned-out larch tree, he found fuel to stay warm and started a fire with the tree pitch he always carried.

Patrick found comfort in his little world. A warm fire, light snow coming down. For dinner, he ate dried elk jerky and cookies from the girls. These days, in the stillness of fresh fallen snow, people called the experience forest bathing.

On the morning of the 22nd, he knew he was a long way from delivering the tree on time. But he vowed to do what he could to keep his promise.

After a meager breakfast, he cut his tree. It was bigger than he remembered. Rope attached and wearing his simple home-made harness, he attempted to move the tree, but it wouldn't budge. Not only was it bigger, it was also a lot heavier than he imagined. After much tugging, the tree finally began to slide down the trail.

"One step then another," he told himself. Old age, cancer, and sore bones made the journey hard, but he kept going. One step, one tug. Over, and over, and over, until he reached the blow down timber.

Patrick struggled to lift the tree over the blow down, but the tree became wedged. No matter how hard he pulled, he couldn't free it.

As daylight faded, doubt crept in. Exhaustion dragged him down, and the shadow in his soul darkened.

"What the hell was I thinking?" He mumbled. "I'm an old man doing stupid things." He sank down on the snow.

Once he was a strong, self-supporting Yaak homesteader. Now he feared he would break his promise to the girls.

Once he believed nothing was impossible. Everything could be done if you work hard enough. Not anymore. He felt as dead as the old blow down he sat on. The darkness deepened around him. He was alone in his world and in his soul.

He had never missed a delivery date.

Until now.

***

As soon as Kathryn returns home, she's on the phone. First calling Kitty on the West Fork who knows most of the new people. Then to Jon who lives upriver from Patrick. The questions are the same. Spread the word. Has anyone seen an old man dragging a tree or a new snowshoe trail?

And the word goes out. New residents, long-time Yaakers, and anyone who hears about Patrick's tree trip checks around their places. Flashlights glow and calls echo in the darkness.

Kathryn is seconds from calling the local rescue group when the phone rings.

***

As Patrick sat surrounded by his shadow of doubt, he began to laugh. "What is wrong with you?" He mumbled. "Sitting here feeling sorry for yourself when the girls need their tree."

His wife would have said, "You're a Yaak homestead man, just get it done."

He rose, put on his headlamp, ignored his weariness, and pondered how to free his stuck tree.

A light glimmered in the darkness.

"Hello up there," a voice said.

"Hello back at you," Patrick responded. Who could be out in the dark besides himself?

As the light moved closer, he saw two people with headlamps on.

"Hello there, name's KC and this is my wife, Cary. We were just out for a little snowshoe walk and saw your light. Looks like you could use a hand. Mind if we help? Not doing much else."

At first Patrick just stared at his new friends. Are they for real? He wondered. Am I seeing things?

The shadow of depression and loneliness lifted, replaced with the hope that maybe he wasn't alone after all.

"Name's Patrick," he finally said, confused but relieved. "Sure could use a hand."

Together the three of them freed the Christmas tree and started down the trail. Going was a little easier than before. When they reached their truck at the road crossing, KC and Cary offered him a cup of hot cocoa from a beat-up Stanley thermos and a few of Cary's Snickerdoodle cookies. Creeping shadows of self-doubt faded into a distant memory.

KC finished his cocoa and asked, "How about we load up your tree and give you a ride home?"

"Thanks kindly but I must finish the way I started," Patrick said. "It's just how l am."

"Mind if I join you?" KC said. "We're new around here and would like to get to know some people."

The offer surprised Patrick. What kind of person would want to drag a tree in the dark? The answer came to him: My kind. "Be much appreciated."

They attached another rope. KC asked Cary to head home and get the word out that Patrick was okay and see if anyone else wanted to drag a tree in the dark. They headed out, pulling the heavy Grand Fir.

***

A phone call from a woman Kathryn doesn't know relieves her. But she still worries about her old neighbor who's fighting cancer. What was he thinking? She wonders. Time for more phone calls.

"Anyone want to help drag a tree in the dark?"

Apparently, yes.

As word goes out about Patrick's location and what he's doing, a funny thing happens. Those who live near the tree trail show up in the dark. One headlamp, then two, then more. More ropes are added. The one-man tree sled becomes a team of many. Old Yaakers, new Yaakers, new friends and old, and anyone who cares about Patrick. Some bring Christmas cookies to share.

After a bit, there's barely enough room left for Patrick to hang on.

In that special early morning light as the sun first sparkles on fresh snow, a human sled team breaks trail across Kathryn's pasture, dragging a good-sized tree. The others make sure Patrick is in the lead.

December 23rd.

Kathryn and the girls embrace him.

"Sorry I'm late," is all he says.

They hustle him into the house and a warm chair.

As Kathryn serves fresh coffee cake and coffee to the sled team, she can't help but laugh. The tree is too big to get through the door, let alone stand up inside the house.

"Let's put it in the yard," little Elly Star suggests. "It belongs to the valley."

This sled team seizes on her idea. In no time, they chip a hole in the ground, stand the tree up, and secure it.

A potluck tree lighting is planned for that evening after everyone gets some rest. People come by to see Patrick and his tree and bring homemade ornaments to hang on it. Light snow gives it a coating of sparkling sugar.

At dusk, they light bonfires and turn on the tree lights. It shines in all its glory for the valley to see.

Kathryn and Patrick sit on the porch, drinking whiskey and

branch water, and watch the gathering of new and old friends.

Kathryn says, "People are calling it Patrick's tree."

"That's nice of them," Patrick answers. "But see all those old timers, new timers, old friends and new friends having a good time around that tree? Elly is right, it's really their tree, the valley's tree." Patrick sips his whiskey and smiles.

A day late but he still delivered.

PART TWO: CHAPTER EIGHT
The Yard Sale

"Excuse me, how much for this?" Says an older voice.

Kathryn turns to see a woman standing at the table that holds the few remaining yard sale items. Not much left after a busy weekend at the ranch and Kathryn is ready to be done.

"How much do you want for this old thermos?" The woman asks again.

Kathryn focuses on that old green, beat-up thermos as a tidal wave of memories floods over her.

Back to that summer when she was little. The summer when she and her mom earned extra money for a special gift for her dad. Baby-sitting, bake sales, selling eggs, and whatever else for a few extra pennies.

For a gypo logging family in the Yaak, there were few extra pennies. An independent logger didn't get paid until a price was negotiated, a tree was cut, limbed, loaded on a truck and off-loaded at the mills. Even back then, trees didn't come easy.

During the process, the equipment that the logger needed would break at some point. Skidders, chokers, loaders, chainsaws, and, of course, log trucks. Everything was expensive and big and doomed to break.

The checks from the mill never seemed to be enough because equipment came first. If you couldn't log, you couldn't work. The family and the ranch came afterward. Not many vacations for gypo logging families.

One thing was missing from Kathryn's dad's inventory of logging gear and she and her mom hoped to fix this.

She still remembers that drive down river with her mom to Gamble's in Troy to pick up the gift they'd ordered weeks before. Her mom let her count out the quarters and rumpled dollar bills.

"It's a secret present for my dad," Kathryn told the clerk.

"My lips are sealed," the clerk replied.

Christmas could not come soon enough for Kathryn and her mom. When Dad opened his special gift, his eyes said it all. A sparkle and maybe a little tear of joy.

His logging gear was complete with a new Stanley Thermos. A true working person's thermos. Large enough to hold a day's worth of coffee but with a small drinking cup. Enough to warm you up but not too much to make you linger. Then back to work!

Kathryn still remembers the first time her mom washed it then set on the counter filled with hot water to preheat it before pouring in his coffee. This routine had been part of morning life for as long as she could remember.

When you work in the woods, it is all about not getting stabbed by broken sticks. It's about having the right gear, from tall leather boots with nails in the soles and tied in the back with knots, no loops to trip on. High cut-off pants and that Hickory zippered shirt. No pant legs or buttons to snag. And of course, a dented metal hard hat. Staying upright as much as possible is the key to a good day in the woods.

And the thermos. Kathryn imagined his pride the first time he broke it out on the job. The ribbing and jokes from the crew were worth it. So was the hot joe from that indestructible thermos. Made from stainless steel with a solid cork plug. Like logging equipment, it was tough.

Her dad and that thermos were never apart. Best friends for sure. Logging days. Fishing days. Working on the ranch days. Or just sitting by the river doing a little morning casting with a hot cup of joe.

Over the years, everyday use wore off the newness. Scratches and dents came with pride, like the time he was running a dozer on the Caribou Fire. The thermos fell onto the dozer tracks, and he backed over it. Luckily it sank in the mud, buried and dented but the coffee was still hot.

Another time, it fell out of his horse's pack saddle on the way to the West Fork elk hunting camp and he didn't notice until he reached camp. He'd hiked back in the dark until he found it in the creek. More dents but the coffee was still warm.

As time went on, that beat-up old green thermos became the family historian that recorded their life in the Yaak. From the logging units it worked. To the fires it went on. To ice fishing at Vinal Lake with Kathryn. To the meetings with other local foresters where it joined the reunion of green thermoses.

Logging was good for Kathryn's family and enabled her to go to college in Missoula.

But it was hard on her father. One logging injury after another finally wore him down. He passed while she was in college. His death devastated her. There was still so much she wanted to do with her pop.

After the funeral, Kathryn offered to quit school and stay at the ranch to help, but her mom was adamant that she should finish college. She agreed but asked for one memento to take with her— that old beat-up green thermos. She needed the memories it held.

True healing from a heart-breaking loss only begins when the good memories surface. Ones that make you smile and maybe laugh a little. Like the first time her dad gave her a sip of coffee from the thermos. She'd hated the taste. That memory made her laugh. With that simple laugh, a wounded heart began to heal.

She didn't use the thermos every day but, on those special fly-fishing days on the Bitterroot or Blackfoot Rivers, she always carried it.

When Kathryn and her new husband moved back to the Yaak and the ranch, that dented, scratched, worn thermos found its way back on the counter where it all began, mainly used for early morning coffee along the river and morning casting.

As time moved on, they started a family and the old thermos was replaced with baby bottles, shifted from the counter and into the pantry where it had been forgotten until now.

"Excuse me." The older woman's voice interrupts Kathryn's daydreams. She's holding the old thermos. "I was asking how much you might want for this."

"I'm sorry, it's not for sale," Kathryn replies. "Not sure how it got out here. It belonged to my logger father and carries a few memories, that's for sure."

"Oh. Okay." The woman sets the thermos back on the table. "I can tell it has some history behind it. My grandson just got his first winter logging job working the Knotty Pine timber sale and I was thinking a thermos like that might be nice to have. I can't afford a new one for him but thanks anyway." She turns to leave.

"Hold on there." Kathryn raises one hand. "You want to give this to your grandson who is going into logging?"

Hope lifts the woman's voice. "His grandfather was a logger, and he wants to give it a try."

"How about free?" Kathryn smiles. "My dad would be pleased his old thermos is going to a young generation of loggers. I know I am."

History continues, kept warm in a dented thermos.

PART TWO: CHAPTER NINE

It Could Be Out There

"It could be out there," little Elizabeth Star says to her mom.

"What's that, dear?" Kathryn asks.

"It really could be out there, Mom," Elly Star says again.

"Oh honey, it's broad daylight and nothing's going to hurt you out there." Kathryn smiles at her oldest daughter but also knows that any number of critters could be out there.

"Don't worry, dear," Kathryn adds. "I can watch you from here."

Even the simplest journey is terrifying the first time. And this is Elly's first time running solo. She's getting to be a big girl, she'd told her mom, and she wants to prove it.

"I can watch you from here and there's nothing out there."

"But it could be out there, so you'll watch, right, Mom?" Ellie Star's furrowed brow asks for reassurance.

"I'm right here watching."

Taking a deep breath, Elly takes her first steps in personal freedom and heads out the door to begin her short but significant journey.

Ninety-nine percent of Americans never make this epic journey. But for those who live in remote places, it's part of daily life.

For homesteaders everywhere, once they find a place to live, their first job is to dig a hole to poop in. The outhouse privy is born.

Outhouse just outside Yaak, MT. Photo by BJ Johnson.

Straightforward in purpose and simple in design, this unique structure is a vital part of remote rural life.

Important decisions go into building an outhouse. At the top of the list: location, location, location. You can't dig a hole just anywhere in the Yaak because Rocky Mountain boulders litter the ground. Can't be too close to the house nor too far away. Nowhere near the water source. Not in the front yard. Usually, out the back door near the woodshed or in the trees. Morning sun or afternoon sun?

The design might not sound like a big deal, but it is. Sloped roof or peaked roof? What protects it best from the elements? No one likes a wet seat. An outhouse full of snow is misery.

The appearance of an outhouse usually matches the personality of the owner. Some are four plain walls and a bench. Depending on the size of the family, others have a deluxe double seater, his and hers.

Many people feel since they spend so much time there, the outhouse should have personality. Some are painted with flowers and trees. Reclaimed windows are installed for light. Posters decorate interior walls. Reading material is a must. The Farmer's Almanac was designed with a hole in it so it can be hung from a string to be read and used in this place of meditation and thought.

Another great debate—door or no door? Some like it closed and secured for privacy. With a door, you can cut the classic quarter moon in it. Others use a curtain, giving the choice of looking out for the chance to see roaming critters.

Mice force you to keep toilet paper in a covered coffee can. The food chain must be considered. Many creatures eat mice. On occasions, a black tail weasel may stop by with its beautiful white winter coat and black on the tip of its tail. In summer, a pair of least weasels run around your feet to see what you're reading and thinking about. Incredibly cute and curious.

There's no getting around the smell. In a well-maintained privy, waste is covered in wood ashes or lime after use. Not all are well-maintained.

There is nothing nice to be said at all about a frozen outhouse in the dead of winter. Some folks take their toilet seat inside the house to keep it warm between uses.

If you have running water in your home, Montana law states that an outhouse is illegal. Still, many people retain an outhouse for memories, a place of refuge, or when the power goes out, which is often in the area.

The Yaak is unique in the world of outhouses because of chance encounters with large meat-eating predators on the way. Grizzly bears, wolves, and mountain lions all roam the wild lands.

Although there are no reported attacks on humans, try convincing little tykes of this. Most are positive that scary wild critters lie in wait to snatch them up as if they're cute little meat packets.

Truth be told, there is some logic behind this concern. Big and small, critters are out there.

Kids develop their own special take on the best times to go to the outhouse.

"All the scary ones go to bed when it gets dark so that's the best time to go. And always go together." This theory shows definite logic.

An opposite view: "Scary ones only come out at night so only go during daylight." If you've ever seen red eyes stare back at you in the dark, this position also sounds logical.

Little folks know how to cover all the bases.

When Kathryn watches her young daughters going alone to the privy for the first time, she laughs to herself. Until their drain field on the ranch is upgraded, the outhouse is the only option.

On little Elly's epic solo journey, she receives a morning hello from a family of robins nesting under the eaves of the outhouse. A northern long-toed salamander offers to share his bench with her.

Elly is right.

Something could be out there.

And it probably is.

PART TWO: CHAPTER TEN

Searching for Mothers

"It's gonna hurt, isn't it?" Little Aspen Rose peers at her mother. "It looks like it's going to hurt."

"I'm sure it's okay and it probably won't feel a thing," Kathryn tells her youngest daughter, smiling inside over the girl's honest concern.

As Kathryn presses the tip in and slowly turns the point, little Aspen says again, "Sure looks like it's going to hurt."

One turn at a time, the slim metal tube, inserting itself.

"When we're done, it won't even know we were here," Kathryn tells Aspen. "It will heal itself in time."

"But, Mom," Aspen protests, "you tell us all living things have feelings and that we should be kind to all living things. And that all things are connected somehow, right?"

"Yes, dear, that's what I believe."

"Well, if that has feelings, I think it's gonna hurt." Aspen's opinion sounds certain.

Kathryn slowly backs out the thin metal tube, pleased that the increment borer didn't break off in the aspen tree.

"More history of the mothers," she tells Aspen as she carefully packages the sample.

Her older daughter Elizabeth Star asks, "How many mothers are there, Mom?"

"Not as many as there used to be. For years the loggers went after the biggest trees. Let's hope we can find a few left. We are looking for as many as we can to record their history." Kathryn adds, "It's our family project."

White pine along the Yaak River.

She believes in teaching her daughters about their home in the Yaak. Bird books, plant books, and books on wildlife cover their kitchen table. And, of course, plenty of books on trees.

Kathryn knows her daughters are still too young to understand how unique and special their wildland world is and how lucky they are to live here even with its hardships and long winters. She wants to teach them that there were very few places with this wide variety of fauna and flora, its wildlife, its abundant water, and most of all, its massive forest.

The forest of trees is unique to itself. Western larch, alpine larch, white bark pine, western red cedar, ponderosa pine, lodgepole pine, white pine, hemlock, Douglas fir, spruce, grand fir, sub-alpine fir, aspen, and birch all grow together as if they are one family unit.

In the world of foresters and lovers of trees, there is a belief that all trees are connected through fungus in their roots. They support each other through good times and bad times and share their natural histories.

Research done by Canadian foresters shows that stands of Douglas fir demonstrate the ability to communicate with each other. Some forest ecologists speak of Mother Trees, matriarchal trees that hold the historical records. They guide younger saplings through their growing years. Like most families, mothers are considered the glue that holds a forest ecosystem together.

Mother trees, or hub trees as they are sometimes called, are the oldest and biggest of any forest group. But, after years of logging the big wood, how many mothers are left?

Kathryn wants to learn as much as she can about the Yaak's history.

And its history is found in the Mother Trees. Drought years, rainy years, growing years, and burning years. Kathryn and her daughters find and record everything they can.

The Yaak, with its massive forest, should have a lot of mother trees but two major factors, logging and fires, reduced their numbers to only isolated islands of trees.

Lumber mills want big wood and loggers love big wood. Over the years, many big trees have been taken to build America.

Fires are the other major factor. In the world of wildland firefighting, the Yaak is known as the asbestos district because of its wet habitat. It generally does not have a lot of fire activity. But, when conditions are right, fires have the potential to become huge due to the heavy timber stands.

The 1910 fire burned over 200,000 acres. In the 1990s, two large fires burned 22,000 acres. The more recent Davis Mountain fire burned over 25,000 acres in the Northwest Peak area.

In the seventies and eighties, a massive mountain pine beetle outbreak led to destruction of lodgepoles followed by major timber sales. Further, the J. Neil's lumber company had clear-cut most of the upper Yaak valley.

These events make finding old mothers a challenge.

Pockets of timber still exist that have not burned or been logged. This is where Kathryn searches for the oldest and biggest mothers.

If one believes in the concept of mother trees, does every tree type have its own mother? There is documentation that stands of aspens are ruled by a mother tree. Does that mean there are lodgepole mothers? Western larch mothers? Spruce mothers?

Figuring out the age of mother trees means coring the tree with an increment borer and counting its growth rings. Coring is the reason for Aspen Rose's concern that the process hurts.

The girls don't yet have the strength to turn the increment borer handles but Kathryn makes sure they do the measuring.

Believing in the concept of mother trees leads to a belief that the forest is a single-family unit with each tree type serving roles in the "family."

Lodgepole pine, birch, aspen, cottonwoods, and western larch are the healers, the first to come back after a fire or logging. They provide shelter and nutrients for trees that follow.

A neighbor had directed Kathryn, Elizabeth, and Aspen to an aspen with a 30-inch DBH (Diameter at Breast Height) in the lower Yaak. Elizabeth and Aspen found a birch tree near Seventeen Mile Creek with a DBH of 45.3 inches that had started to grow after the 1910 fire.

Cedars are the keepers of the story of the river and creek bottoms. Long-lived, they dwell in cool river bottoms. They survive while hills around them have burned and been logged. They stay protected to preserve the history of the river family around them.

Kathryn's neighbor Patrick led them to a hidden western red cedar living on the river that somehow survived early logging. With a 118.2-inch DBH, it's too big to core.

Mighty hemlock trees in the Yaak collect the forest's worries and carry them in their hanging limbs. Their tops hang like bowed heads. They may be mighty, but they don't live long—they rot quickly because of the heavy load they bear.

The beautiful spruce is the sanctuary tree, the protector of small wildlife. Birds, chipmunks, squirrels and many more find shelter in its tight branches with sharp needle-like leaves. The girls found a spruce tree that was 33.9 inches DBH. Kathryn read about a Norway spruce that is 9500 years old. That's one old mother.

Of course, every family has its royalty, those that stand above, like the majestic white pine. Huge at its base and towering over its subjects in all its glory. A changing world has not been kind to these magnificent rulers. Disease is taking its toll. The family is slowly losing another part of its history.

At one of her favorite fishing spots along the river, Kathryn measured a white pine with a 76-inch DBH that's too big to core.

Every family has its own guardians, the survivors, like ponderosa pine, that some call yellow pine. They stand tall on southern hillsides surviving summer fires and winter storms. They absorb all the elements in their gnarled rough bark while protecting the history they hold inside. A ponderosa pine on Seventeen Mile Creek started growing right after the 1910 fire. It is now more than 112 years old, with a **DBH** of 38.9 inches.

For a family to survive, it needs worker bees that are everywhere. They provide nutrients, shade, and spread family gossip through their roots. Douglas fir is the only tree named after a human. While not as long lived as some, they provide the ingredients for a forest to thrive.

Grand fir contributes to the unique smell of the forest family. Some locals call it the piss fir because it spits pitch when you drill it with an increment borer. It dwells with cedar and hemlock in the cool wetlands of the Yaak.

There is always one family member that stands out, the one everyone loves. The western larch, also called the tamarack. The healer and survivor, the guardian and provider. The aged keeper of the long story of the Yaak.

The Yaak is blessed with some of the highest concentrations of this unique, beautiful tree. In the fall, it shows pride in the family by sharing its golden glory to all those around it.

During a hike into the upper Yaak Wood Creek Larch Scenic Area, Kathryn and the girls measured and cored a larch with a 37.5 inches DBH. They could only drill three-quarters of the way before hitting rot. They stopped so they wouldn't lose the bit deep inside the trunk. Fifteen out of the almost 19-inch radius revealed 308 years. This tree is probably 400 years old. A survivor.

Kathryn teaches the girls about the family member that holds the ancient history of the Yaak—the alpine larch of the high country. They grow in the harsh high elevations of northwest peaks in solidarity stands that are not connected to other root systems. They survive for hundreds of years in some of the harshest environments Montana has to offer. Local foresters say these isolated survivors may be 1000 to 1500 years old, truly the family historians that keep their forest story alive.

On a hike into Hawkins Lake for high lake fishing and tree searching, Kathryn and her daughters measured four alpine larch trees. The largest trees had rotted a few inches in. They cored 14-inch DBH in a healthy alpine larch, and learned it was 425 years old. It had been born around 1600, the same time the English founded the Jamestown colony.

If there was ever an ultimate queen mother to others, it must be the white bark pine tree. Like the alpine larch, living and surviving in the harsh rocky high places of the Yaak, it provides nutrients to all. The first to come in and long lived, it shelters the seedlings that follow. It is a food source for many creatures.

This unique mother can only grow when its seeds are harvested and buried by a bird called the Clark's Nutcracker. These seed stashes become a critical food source for creatures from squirrels to grizzly bears.

Like all mothers in the changing Yaak world, they are aging, and their numbers are declining. At Hawkins Lake, the girls could only bore four inches before hitting rot in a 30-2 DBH white bark pine. Soon another important family member will be lost.

Past forest fires and logging dictate the age of trees in certain areas. In places affected by the 1910 fires, the trees now growing range from 100 to 110 years old, still young in terms of forest history.

From the sheltered cedar woods of Meadow Creek, where the caribou came for protection to give birth, to the high ridge-line of alpine larch surrounding Hawkins Lake, these mothers hold the forest family's true history and preserve their legacy.

"If there are momma trees, are there papa trees, too?" Elizabeth Star asks.

"There must be, dear." Kathryn sweeps her arm across the view. "Look at all the baby trees everywhere. When we're done with the Mother Trees, we'll start looking for the Master Trees."

The search for history never ends.

***

Finding the Mother Tree by Suzanne Simard is a good reference if you believe in the concept.

PART TWO: CHAPTER 11

Leaving God's Country

It was barely audible, a simple sigh from Kathryn's neighbor and dear friend Patrick, dozing in the passenger seat.

Was it a sigh of relief? A sigh of frustration for all he's gone through? Or a sigh of recognition? As they crossed the Purcell Divide and headed down the curves of Smoot Creek, maybe he knew home wasn't too far away now.

After many trips, Kathryn could almost drive this road with her eyes closed. But, during recent midnight runs to the emergency room in Libby, additional passengers of dread and concern had hitched a ride.

The Pipe Creek Road. A lifeline to Libby for those who lived remotely. A log truck road, named after the local stones that Native Americans used in making their pipes. The J. Neils lumber company built it, and the St. Regis lumber company improved it to access their Yaak timber holdings. The road led to the location of the tree that had once been chosen as the national Christmas tree, now only a stump left behind.

Kathryn chuckles to herself when she hears new folks

complaining about road conditions or the lack of plowing in winter. She still remembers many winters it never got plowed. If the mills weren't logging in the Yaak that winter, it didn't get plowed.

Back then, the one-lane 508 to Bonners Ferry was the lifeline, if and when the county got around to plowing it.

Kathryn had grown increasingly concerned about her neighbor. After his Christmas tree adventure, he never regained his strength and energy. She's noticed a dimming of the sparkle in his eyes.

She'd known Patrick as long she'd been alive. After her father passed suddenly, Kathryn and her mom were left to deal with everyday life on the ranch. Patrick and his wife Anne stepped up and started a local support group of neighbors.

Little things. A cord of larch firewood dropped off without a word. A loaf of homemade bread with a jar of huckleberry jam on the front porch. A dozen fresh eggs in the mailbox. Those little things got them through the heartache.

Now it was Kathryn's turn to help her neighbor.

A few years before, his wife had passed. Patrick continued to maintain the homestead on his own, but it wasn't easy. Emotional loss combined with the physical labor of ranching took a toll.

If Kathryn had her way, she'd take Patrick to her place so she and the girls could watch over him until he got better.

Not to be. After a week at the hospital in Kalispell, the stubborn old coot wanted to sleep in his own bed.

***

Patrick wasn't really dozing. It just took less energy to leave his eyes closed. As they crossed the divide and started down into the Yaak, he let out a little sigh of recognition. Home was getting closer by the mile.

Memories of times past filled his head. Bushwhacking their way into the beaver ponds of Smoot Creek looking for cutthroat trout. Stopping at the Cherokee Strip for a darn good burrito, a beer cooled by a mountain stream, and an update on the latest gossip. Now only memories buried under a pile of ashes.

His few remaining peers often complained that getting old sucked. But not Patrick. Getting old was just the way it was. If you didn't get old, you didn't get memories—the good and the bad. Elk hunting with friends and whiskey around the campfire. Moonlight talks with Anne sitting alongside the river. Worries about the winter's grubstake and property taxes. The good and the bad.

For the first time in his life, Patrick felt weariness in his bones. The midnight runs to the hospital ER in Libby, the blood transfusions to keep him alive, then finally the emergency surgery to figure out what was wrong.

Somehow, he found the strength to survive two bouts of cancer. But where did the strength come from to survive the treatments themselves?

They told him, We stopped the cancer, but sorry, the treatments are killing you slowly.

Hospitalization was all right for healing, but terrible for rest.

He'd always been a wanderer and lately he wandered the hospital ward in the middle of the night, listening to various memories, as some faded away. What memories did he have to pass on?

The Homestead was everything. Patrick and Anne believed if you cared for your land, your land would care for you. Simple rules for a homesteader in the day. Don't overgraze your pastures. Take what timber you need but replant twice as much. Don't kill more than you can keep. Keep the stock out of the ponds and streams because clean water was the lifeline for a ranch.

From day one on the homestead there were no days off. Chores always needed doing.

But there were also those special times that made all the work worthwhile. Early morning coffee watching elk in the morning fog in the lower pasture. Evening casting for redbands in the river as the alpenglow lit the surrounding mountains.

Patrick knew his time on the ranch was coming to an end. Long ago, he'd chosen to live in a remote place for independence, the independence to be oneself. But that was slipping from his grasp. If it weren't for Kathryn and a few others, he'd be in serious trouble. Since Anne's passing, work became harder and the joy they'd shared together on the ranch faded.

Montana law allows you to be buried on your property. He and Anne had surveyed out a place for a family plot along the river. She'd been laid to rest in her native flower garden. Sooner or later, he would be joining her.

But not right now. There were still tasks that needed to be done. A wood stove to light, firewood to haul, always something.

And he had to decide what to do with the ranch.
***

As Kathryn pulls into Patrick's driveway, as she's done countless times before, the simple beauty of the place awes her. Beside the river is a beautiful log home. Stones hauled from the river form the foundation and the house is constructed from huge western larch logs cut from the homestead. Everything is neat and tidy and in its place. Cleared pastures and meadows stretching along the river give the home open views of the Purcell Mountains all around. One beautiful place.

When they reach the house, they find the wood stove already lit, firewood stacked, and fresh food in the fridge. Patrick had helped many a neighbor over the years and now it's payback time. Kathryn had called ahead, and this is what neighbors do.

Kathryn gives Patrick a goodbye hug and reminds him to call without hesitation for anything.

***

Patrick was home again. The smell of home brought even more memories back. Time to stop. He poured himself a little scotch, with lots of water, as his doctors told him. And only one. They had great concerns about sending him back to the remote Yaak in his present condition, but home was the best healer. There was no place like his deck chair surrounded by the world he loved.

The land spread out before him, meadows and pastures that he and Anne toiled over for years. First, they used horses to pull out stumps then later a beat-up pickup. When people commented on the beautiful meadows, he laughed to himself because he knew a layer of stumps still lay not far under.

He'd been struggling with how much the Yaak had changed in the last few years. In the past, his place had always been open to neighbors and friends. But a couple of years ago, for the first time ever, he had to put up a gate because strangers kept showing up, wanting to buy his place. Hard to believe the offers they made because he remembered how badly property values had dropped in the seventies and eighties after the logging died.

Now his friend Kitty, who sold local real estate, was telling him he could probably get one to two million dollars for the ranch, as is. He laughed, thinking what Anne would have said about that. How many mason jars does it take to bury a million dollars? She never trusted banks.

Patrick remembered the Yaak as a place where a person could make a living working in the woods. He had done all kinds of jobs over the years, from timber cutter to tree planter. For a while, they even had a mill, cutting lumber for local homes. Working in the woods created the world he had now.

But a working Yaak was a relic of the past. It saddened him that this place he called home and earned his livelihood for most of his life had become nothing more than a marketing tool for environmental groups to raise money from back east. Their rallying cry: "Save the Yaak so only we can use it."

After years of clear cutting, maybe that wasn't a bad thing. Still...

Grizzly saviors had also approached him. At first, he liked their mission but soon grew concerned about their selfish ways. Didn't seem right to him that they bought up land and restricted access to only the rich. Give us a thousand dollars and we'll let you walk along our creek.

He remembered back when a grizzly tag only cost a buck and they were hunted until they were almost gone. That didn't sit right with him either. He liked seeing them but didn't trust them and never wanted to shoot one.

Now, developers dreamed of subdividing as many lots as possible to maximize their investment. They advertised private hunting lodges with river views to out-of-state buyers. That left little space for the elk that spent the spring in the upper meadows.

These days, being a builder was tough and he knew many a local carpenter who could use the work. He didn't like losing fishing spots to new homes, but work was work.

Patrick wasn't money rich, just land rich, and getting old was expensive. Eventually he'd have to sell the place to cover his future costs, even though he's rather give the whole place to Kathryn and the girls for all they'd done for him.

Where to go was another problem. Like most small communities in Montana, assisted living homes were nonexistent. Missoula and Spokane were the only current options and cost up to seventy thousand a year.

Expensive and a long way from home.

A person had few chances to own property and once it was sold, it was gone.

Times like this, he missed his partner the most. Anne's steady train of thought and ability to see through the clutter at times helped his craziness.

"All things in due time," he mumbled and sipped his whiskey.

He still had a few more early morning coffees with the elk and Rocky Mountain alpenglow sunsets to share with Anne in her flowers.

When he finally did sell, Kathryn would get a new pickup and the girls would have college costs covered. It's what neighbors do for all they'd done.

Patrick closed his eyes in the comfort of his little world, knowing he wasn't leaving god's country quite yet.

He let out a barely audible sigh.

A sigh of home.

PART TWO: CHAPTER TWELVE

It's a Mystery

"Whatcha think, early miner maybe?" The dozer operator asks his crew. They stare down at a pile of arranged rocks. "Back in the day, miners wandered everywhere around here."

"Nah, more likely a homesteader who probably starved out like most of them did," the backhoe operator says. "Once all the game got killed off, wasn't much left to eat. Probably died from consumption. Yep, a homesteader for sure."

Kathryn stands at the rear of the group of construction workers, holding her stop sign. She says, "The state survey folks say it might be Native American."

"You mean an Indian, Indian?" someone asks.

The crew boss says, "Good thing you noticed those rocks, Katy. Wouldn't be right, putting a highway on top of someone's grave, no matter who it is."

It's 1989 and Kathryn has scored a summer job as a road flagger on the dead man's curve road reconstruction. Not the most exciting work in the world, but, as a federal highway job, the money is great. That will really help with college and maybe even new skis.

Plus, it's close to home so she can help around the ranch after work. And, of course, enjoy a little evening river casting.

Kathryn is there every day at the 22.5 mile marker on State Highway 508, enduring rain, wind, hail, dust, blazing summer heat, and the endless girly jokes from the log truck drivers. Being born and raised in the Yaak, she knows most of the people coming through and hears lots of gossip.

A lot of the time, she just stares at the world around her. That's when she notices a simple pile of stones. On her lunch break, she pulls weeds until she finds a mound surrounded by a ring of stones. It has to be a grave.

Survey stakes extend out past the site, like they plan to bury it under the new road.

She has to speak up.

State surveyors arrive to inspect it then leave to decide what to do.

Now the workers wait.

Someone asks, "They gonna dig it up and move it?"

"Not sure, up to the state folks now," the crew boss says. "Let's head upriver. We'll work on that curve until we find out." He faces Kathryn. "And, Katy, tell them damn log trucks to slow down. Kinda tight at the curve."

The dozer operator climbs up to his seat and mumbles, "It's a mystery for sure, by gum."

***

When he volunteered, he told himself he would stay to the end, no matter the outcome. He was a man of his word and he stayed to the end.

The fight was over. He was one of the few to survive the endless, bloody carnage without major injuries. But he was broken, physically worn out, and mentally exhausted.

All he had left were the clothes on his back, a well-worn hunting rifle, and two good feet. He could still walk, so walk he did, one foot in front of the other.

At first, he walked with the other survivors, but one by one, they filtered off to their own lives until he was alone.

He kept walking.

Word had spread about gold being discovered in the Montana territory and a chance at free land to those who could work it. He heard it was where the Rocky Mountains reached the sky. So walk he did.

***

Growing up in the Yaak, Kathryn knew of many abandoned homesteads with graves from the first adventurers into this country. Her father took her to visit them. "They worked too hard to get to this place to be forgotten," he said as they pulled up weeds and cleaned the graves.

Most were just a pile of stones around the mounds. A few had etchings of dates, sometimes even a name. Neatly arranged stones for forgotten souls in the wilderness.

Her father told her, "The Yaak can be a harsh place. If you let it, long winters and loneliness weaken you. Don't fight the Yaak. Embrace this home we have, treat it fairly, and it will give us all we need."

As Kathryn works her traffic control duties, she wonders who is buried under the stones. She spends her lunch breaks having little talks with her new friend in the grave.

"Are you a man or woman? What's your name? When did you come here?"

Kathryn stares at the surroundings. "Bet you could tell a story or two about how you ended up in a beautiful flower-covered meadow beside a river flowing by."

***

Work was where he found it. A day's labor for a meal or two.

With the war over, the west was expanding. Railroads, mines, and new towns popped up, offering as much work as he could take.

He worked long enough to resupply his grubstake and then kept walking. Along the way, he told others, "Gotta see where the Rocky Mountains touch the sky in that Montana territory."

One day, he walked into the Rocky Mountain gold fields of Helena, Montana. After years of fighting and bloody violence in the war, the rowdy world of miners was not for him.

His wounded soul needed a wildflower meadow by a Montana river. "Just keep walking, left foot, then the right." Mile after mile.

***

As word spread of the gravesite find, those in charge didn't know what to do. "It's just another dead homesteader's grave. No one really cares," some said. "We should just shut up and bury it."

Others said, "What if it's a civil war veteran? There were a lot of those folks around here back in the day. Can't abuse a veteran's grave."

"Maybe a Native American," says someone else. "They used to have summer camps all up and down the river. No one cares about them."

Kathryn cares.

***

As he walked westward, he crossed MacDonald Pass down onto the Cokahalishkit (Blackfoot) River. Coming from the Great Plains, he saw more water than he ever imagined, from the Blackfoot to the Clark Fork River.

He heard about northern gold fields and railroad work up on the Aqkinmiluk (Kootenai) River in a mining town called Sylvanite. And free land for those who could work it. That called him farther north.

***

Coming from a line of early settlers, Kathryn knows the struggles and hardships of trying to make it in a place like this Yaak. The winter isolation that drove people to wackiness. The short growing seasons meant the chance of starvation was always present. Many early settlers failed for those reasons. She understood and at times felt their pain. For the hardships they endured, she thought their graves should be treated with respect. Natives or white settlers, both shared the same struggles and joy of this place.

So, she was relieved when the state archives people, surveyors, and others decided to move the whole road a little to the left.

***

He walked up the Bull River Valley to the Kootenai River and log ferry at the railroad stop of Yahk. During the last miles north along the Yaak River, he still couldn't imagine a place like this. Water flowing down everywhere. Trees taller than any building he had ever seen. And the smell of life, of growing things. He didn't know that many wildflowers bloomed in the whole world.

The booming mining town of Sylvanite offered work for awhile but not the rest his spirit craved. He was not yet done walking.

At the assay office he learned that, for fifty dollars, four stakes at the corners, and the will to work, he could claim 160 acres of virgin ground upriver. He walked a little farther until he found his flower-covered meadow by a river. He staked the corners, paid his fifty dollars, and sat by the river in the meadow of his new land.

The walking man was done. He was now a homestead man.

***

"Mom, why do you always wave at that spot?" Ellie Star asks Kathryn. "There are no cars coming."

They're driving to Bonners Ferry for supplies.

"Just waving at an old friend, honey," Kathryn answers. "It's good to remember our old friends." Especially one friend from the summer of 1989 when she worked as a flagger on the road crew.

"Who is it, Mom? What's their name?"

"No one knows, could be a settler or maybe a Native American. It's a mystery."

***

The road was finished that summer, transformed from a country lane to a busy tourist route. A small fence was installed around the grave of the unknown dead. Sadly, it was later vandalized.

In researching this story, I talked with many locals, people who worked on the road, local tribal, and Montana state folks, as well as searching my own memories. No one knows for certain. Recently I put up a small American flag and some juniper and cedar bows to celebrate their life. Whoever it is.

It's a mystery.

About the Author

Like many of the early homesteaders he writes about, Edd Kuropat was a wanderer. With his partner, Betty they wandered from California to Alaska looking for that special place to create a life together. Then one day they wandered into that special place in western Montana called the Yaak. They had found their home. Edd has a unique connection with the Yaak from building a log home with local trees and stones from the river as a foundation to working as a Wildland Fire fighter, tree planter, timber cutter, carpenter, and finally a maker of artistic furniture and a writer of tales. In his art work and his stories, Edd brings the Yaak to life in a unique interesting ways. His inspiration comes from the world around him. From hiking the many trails to fishing its lakes and many forks of the Yaak River.